Dating Grace

Dedicated to the glory of God—El-Roi, the God who sees me, and in honor of Sister Ginny who told me about life commandments, those dynamics which often dictate our lives, but don't have to; and in honor of parents who have grieved over children they've outlived; and children who were too young when their parents died.

"I will not leave you orphaned; I am coming to you."
–Jesus' words in the Gospel of John 14:18

Dating Grace

Jennifer Johnson

DATING GRACE

Her Good Samaritan needs rescuing though he doesn't know it.

Hospital chaplain Grace Sutton isn't looking for love when she becomes stranded in the middle of nowhere. But when Ches Larson and his 4-year-old niece stop to help her, Grace feels drawn to the gentleman ranger and the adorable child with him.

Raising his teenage daughter and his niece isn't easy especially when Ches knows he's on borrowed time. So when Grace walks into a hospital room and finds Ches is the patient, she has to convince him his life is worth fighting for, so she can be a part of it, too.

Chapter One

Grace Sutton allowed herself a five-minute pity party. A loud chorus of cicadas provided the soundtrack in the deepening shadows of the day. Grace's car rested in a ditch next to a dirt road with nothing around but corn fields and trees. She'd fallen into a mud puddle trying to exit the car, soaking her skirt and dunking her slingback shoes. Attempting to get a signal on her phone to call a tow service, she'd walked in bared feet about thirty yards before she'd cut the bottom of her foot on a rock. Limping back to her car, she sat in the open door and pressed a napkin she'd found in her glovebox to the wound.

At least, she had a good excuse for not going to her cousin's wedding now. With Denise getting married this evening, Grace would be the only female over the age of 18 in the family still single. She'd dreaded the wedding, especially since she hadn't been able to find a date. A week ago, she'd resolutely marked "one" on the rsvp, though the invitation had offered her a "plus one." But there was no way she could go to the wedding *now*.

Grace smiled, and the pity party was over.

I'm so sorry, Denise, I missed your wedding. You see this deer ran out in front of my car, and….

A low rumbling in the distance interrupted Grace's thoughts. It was a car. Relief and trepidation wrestled within her. She was on the side of the road in the midst of cornfields and not much else. A vulnerable place to be. She looked at the screen of her phone again. Still no signal.

Lord, keep me safe.

The sound grew louder, and a truck pulling a horse trailer crested the hill going at a steady pace. The driver was male and wearing a ball cap. And in the passenger seat was a child in a car seat. The truck slowed and then stopped when it came abreast of her car. A girl with big green eyes stared at Grace through the glass of the window. The engine shut off, and the driver door opened. The man exited the vehicle and walked around it. He wore blue jeans and a navy untucked T-shirt. And cowboy boots. Grace watched the boots approach her, and when he was close, she looked up, up, up.

"Are you all right?" he drawled in a molasses voice.

Tall. He was really tall.

From under the bill of his cap, eyes similar in shade to the little girl in the truck gazed at her and waited.

"Did you ever have one of those days?" she asked.

His lips parted in a smile which creased his cheeks. "Sugar, I have them quite often." He paused, and his eyes shifted to her foot resting on her knee. "What's wrong with your foot?"

"I stepped on a rock. I'm sure it's fine. Small cut, really. I'm just waiting for it to quit bleeding."

Little knuckles rapped on the truck window. The man turned and stepped to the truck door. He opened it.

"Can I get out?" a melodic voice asked, and Grace's heart turned with tenderness.

"I suppose so," he answered sedately.

The child freed her seat belt from the booster seat, and the man helped her down from the truck. She wore pink leggings and a pink sparkly T-shirt with a tutu sewed to the bottom hem. Pink cowboy boots completed the ensemble. Her hair was done up in high pigtails. "Hi. I'm Haley. What's your name?"

"I'm Grace. It's nice to meet you." She held out her hand, and with a giggle Haley shook it. "How old are you, Haley?"

"I'm five years old. How old are you?"

The man clucked his tongue. "You shouldn't ask a lady her age, Little Bit."

"That's okay. I don't mind telling. I'm thirty-two."

"My pop's thirty-eight, ain't you, Pop?"

Pop?

It seemed an unusual name for a dad.

He reached down and picked the girl up and settled her on his arm. "All right now. Don't be telling all my secrets." They looked at each other for a moment then both turned back to her. "What happened?"

"A deer ran out in front of me, and I swerved to miss it."

"A deer," Haley exclaimed.

Grace bent down and held the makeshift gauze to her foot as she placed it on the ground then stood testing her weight on it.

"Whoa! You're big," Haley commented.

"She's tall," he corrected.

"Wicked tall," Haley amended.

"Wicked tall?" Grace glanced at the man. Even at six feet, she had to look up to meet his gaze, something that almost never happened.

"She means in a good way."

"Yeah, a good way. We like tall people, don't we, Pop?"

"Sure, we do. So, have you tried to move your car since you swerved to miss the deer?"

"Yes. It's stuck."

"That why you were walking barefoot on the road?"

"My shoes were wet, and I couldn't get a signal on my phone."

"Would you like me to try to get the car out for you?"

"Yes."

"Before we do that, why don't you sit back down, and I'll tend to your foot. I've got a first aid kit in the truck." He went to the truck and set Haley on her seat.

"It's fine."

"Ooo, you hurt your foot," Haley said. "Let Pop help you. He's good at stuff like that."

Okay then. "Is he?" Grace sat.

He knelt on one knee and placing the kit on the road,

he opened it.

She thought she saw him glance at her wet skirt. Self-consciously, she pulled it away from her legs. "I stepped in a puddle," she said.

"Did you now?" He sorted through the box, picked up a small container, read the label, then put it back.

"I suppose I didn't so much step into the puddle as I slid into it."

"Ah," he commented, nodding.

"I'll do it," Grace said, not wanting him to touch her, wishing she was the kind of girl who had pedicures and small dainty feet.

"All right." He handed her an alcohol swab, and she dabbed it on the cut.

Haley stood next to them with her hands on her hips. "That stuff burns," she said.

"I'm tough. I can take it."

Next he handed her a tube of antibiotic ointment, then a Band-Aid.

"I cry when Pop tries to put that on me, so he just washes my booboos with soap and water."

Tenderness brought a smile to Grace's face. What a beautiful child she was. "It's nice that he'd use soap and water so it doesn't hurt as bad."

"Yeah.... Where you going?"

"A wedding."

Haley gasped, her small mouth open in shock, her eyes wide in delight. "Are you getting married?"

Grace grinned and reached forward to brush the tip of the girl's nose with her finger. "No. My cousin is."

"Aren't you married yet?"

"No, are you?"

"I'm not old enough, and Pop's too old and set in his ways. But we could go to your cousin's wedding. Just to watch."

"I don't think so, Little Bit. You have to be invited to go to a wedding."

"You'd invite us, wouldn't you, Grace?"

"Call her, 'Miss Grace.'"

He scooped up the kit and stood, then held out his hand to her to help her up. His work-roughened fingers grasped hers, and when Grace stood next to him, for the first time since she'd sprung up over her classmates in seventh grade, she felt feminine. Grace looked straight on at the column of his neck, then higher at the whisker-darkened jawline, until she met his eyes shadowed under the bill of his cap. Nice eyes. Kind eyes.

"What's your name?" Grace asked.

"People call me Ches."

Grace resisted the urge to tell him his height made her feel almost short or ask him how tall he was because she knew how it felt to have your height to be your defining characteristic.

"Ches, as in Chester?"

"Ches as in Chesapeake. How's your foot?"

He didn't want to talk about himself. Grace filed away the unusual name in her mind and wondered if she'd ever know the story of it.

"My foot feels better. Thank you." Grace walked to the truck and stood next to the open door beside Haley.

"You're going to the wedding with your skirt wet," the little girl observed.

"Well, I don't know. I was planning on going to the wedding, but I'd be embarrassed to go with wet clothes. I will probably just go back home." Thinking of her great excuse for missing the wedding, Grace smiled again.

"Where's do you live?" Haley asked.

"I live in Carlton. Do you know where that is? It's about 45 minutes north of here."

Haley's forehead wrinkled in thought. "Pop, do we know where Carlton is?"

"We went through there one time when you went to the zoo in Columbus."

"Oh! Yeah! We like that place." The child began to talk about her trip to the zoo. Grace listened with half an ear, but she watched Haley's pop. She'd said he wasn't married because he was too set in his ways. Maybe she wasn't his child at all, but Grace dismissed the thought immediately. The two were too close, too familiar with each other. Whether father or grandfather, Chesapeake was Haley's family.

Ches scratched his chin, making a scraping noise against the beginnings of a beard. "Where's the wedding?"

"Athens City."

"Did you take a wrong turn? We aren't really on the way to Athens City."

"The GPS directed me."

His gaze twinkled. "Shortest route, huh?"

Grace's heart hitched. Oh my goodness, he was handsome. "Apparently."

Ches walked down the embankment, and the door opened. He sat down in the car, and the engine started soon afterward. The tires spun, and the car lurched, but it didn't do much more than that.

Oh, darn it. What now? He sat in the car a few minutes, and Grace bent her head to peer in the vehicle. What was he doing?

In a few minutes, he exited the car and rejoined them.

Grace didn't want to ask him to help her. She didn't want to appear needy and inconvenience anyone, but she was stuck.

"If you'll just take me some place where I can get service on my cell phone, I'll call AAA, and a tow truck will come get me."

Ches shrugged. "I called Jester Mason. He runs the service station in town. He can probably get you out of here, but not before eight."

"Eight?"

"Yeah."

"We'll leave the keys under the mat on the floorboard, and he'll take it to my house."

"Your house?"

"Sure. I live less than a mile from here."

"Perfect! We'll go to the wedding, and by the time we

get back, your car will be ready!" Haley said. She kicked the dashboard. "It's perfect. Perfect. Perfect. Perfect."

Ches's mouth turned up at the corner, and his gaze went from the little girl to her.

He reached into the truck and buckled the seatbelt across her car seat, then he stepped back.

"It will be easier for you to slide across the driver's seat."

Grace stared at him, trying to figure out what he was saying. "I'm sorry. I don't understand."

"You'll have to sit in the middle. It's a bench seat, so it's not too uncomfortable."

"I'm...." She looked down at her skirt. "Wet."

"That's all right, sugar. We can dry your skirt while Little Bit and I are changing clothes."

"Are we going to your house then?"

"Sure. Then we'll head down to your wedding." He walked around the truck and opened the driver's door. Lifting his chin in invitation, he waited, and Grace followed him.

"I couldn't possibly," she said. "I couldn't impose on you. The wedding's in Athens City. That's over an hour away."

He shook his head. "Forty-five minutes."

Grace clutched her purse and shoes to her chest. "I just think...you know... It's too much."

"Why don't you let me take you to the house? We can at least do something about your skirt."

She sighed and sat on the driver's seat then slid over. Ches handed her half of the seat belt, and she felt down in the cushion for the other piece. By the time she had it clicked on her lap, he was beside her, and, boy, was it cozy.

"I think I'll just have to wear a wet skirt. I don't have any clothes to change into."

"You got your big girl panties on, don't cha?" Haley asked.

"Umm... yes." The little girl's question jarred Grace. Yeah, this was about the big girl panties, wasn't it? Dealing with life, and not letting the bumps and curves it threw at her keep her down. "Yes, I do."

Ches started the motor, and the truck moved forward along the road. She wondered what Ches thought about her admitting that she was wearing big girl panties, but he didn't say anything. In a few minutes, he turned down a dirt road in between the corn fields and followed it to a two story wooden house with a big balcony and an even bigger front porch.

"That's our house," Haley said.

"It's lovely," Grace replied.

"Lovey. Yes. It's lovey."

Grace turned to him and waited for him to correct the little girl, but he didn't. He winked. "It *is* lovey," he agreed.

One of the doors of the double garage opened in front of them, but Ches didn't pull inside. Instead he shifted the truck in reverse and backed it next to the garage. "Can you ladies give me a few minutes to unhitch the horse trailer?" He looked at Grace, then at Haley, as if he were actually seeking permission.

"You have a horse?" Grace asked.

"Yeah, but we loaned him out," Haley said. "On account of Mr. Pete's got a horse in season."

Grace wasn't exactly sure what it meant for a horse to be in season, but she could guess, and she felt heat rise from her neck to her face. She faced forward and studied the dashboard. "Please, don't let me hinder you in any way. I really appreciate your help."

"It's my pleasure," he said in that unhurried way of his. "Ma'am."

He can't be real. No one is that gentlemanly, that smooth. Are they?

He opened the door and exited the vehicle. Grace breathed a sigh of relief for the extra space in the cab now. Not that he had crowded her—the truck was plenty big enough—but he was so tall. He had to be at least six seven. His presence even more so. Rugged and outdoorsy, like a man in Hallmark movie.

"What's your horse's name?" Grace asked, amidst metallic noises outside, and motion.

"Lad. He's Pop's horse. He's a real good horse. He's older than I am. I want a pony, but Pop says I have to wait cause he wants to break it hisself, and he says he ain't got time right now. And Cinnamon got gone, and there was heck to pay for it and loosums to tie up, whatever that means. Also, a pony's got to be good stock. You can't just bring any horse home, you know. Pop says he's on the lookout. Plus, I have to be taller, which won't be a problem since I'm the tallest one in my class already. I'm thinking by Christmas, we'll be in business, and what a great present for Santa to bring me. Don't you agree?"

Grace wasn't expecting the sudden pause as the girl waited for her to answer. She didn't want to agree if Ches had no intention of getting the girl a pony for Christmas, and ruminated on a noncommittal answer.

"It seems a pony is rather large to fit in Santa's sleigh."

A crease formed between Haley's brows. "He won't bring it in the sleigh. It'll have to be in a horse trailer. Santa has to work it out with Pop ahead of time."

"Oh."

"Didn't you ever get an animal from Santa?"

"No. Just toys."

"Well, it's complicated when it's livestock what with the freezing temperatures at the North Pole. Didn't you ever think of that?"

"Honestly, no. I never have."

"What's the best thing you ever got from Santa?"

Grace thought back through all of her Christmases at home. "I think it was a doll house with all of the furniture inside and real working lights. It was exquisite."

"Ex-squeeze-it."

"Exquisite. Ex. Squiz. It."

"Ex. Squiz. It. What's it mean?"

"Oh." Grace searched her mind to define the word. "It means beautiful in a delicate way."

"Ooooooh. I like that word. Exquisite. Exquisite."

The driver door opened, and Ches sat down. He moved the gear shift and directed the truck inside garage.

The space next to the truck was empty.

"That's where my sissy parks."

"Your sissy?"

"Yeah. But she's studying tonight. Ain't that right, Pop?"

"That's right. Haley's sissy, my daughter Sunni, is taking some summer courses, and she's studying for a big test."

"And she better do good, too, cause if she fails, she won't get credit for the class, and then what's she going to do?"

Grace smiled. Obviously, Haley was relaying a portion of a conversation she had heard.

"Do you like dogs, sugar?" Ches asked.

"Oh, yes. We always had dogs growing up."

"How come you don't have one now?" Haley asked.

"Well, I had one, but she died, and I'm waiting for another right dog to come along."

"Whatdoyamean?"

"There are a lot of dogs who need homes, so when a dog who needs a home shows up and likes me, then I'll know that's the dog for me."

"Aha. We gots a dog, but that's only because Sissy brought him home, and she and I both cried cause Pop said no."

"Huh." Grace bit her lip to keep from smiling.

"Pop changed his mind, obviously," Ches said. "But not because of all the crying. Jojo's a good dog. But he's big, so if you're uncomfortable, I can put him up before we go inside."

"Oh, I'm sure it's fine."

"He's a sweetheart, ain't he, Pop?"

"A gentle giant, but he is really big."

Haley looked at her Pop. "Well, so is Grace. She ain't umcomferble."

Grace smiled at Haley's attempt at saying *uncomfortable*.

"Let's go then."

Haley unbuckled her seat belt, and they all exited the vehicle. Grace followed Haley into the door, aware that Ches followed behind her. The door opened into a small room with a washer and dryer. A full basket of clothes sat on top of the dryer. Ches walked around her and dug through the clothes. "Here you go," he said handing her a pair of cotton sweat pants. "They're clean. You can wear them until your skirt dries. The bathroom is through there, and Little Bit and I will go upstairs and see you in a few minutes."

Chapter Two

Haley pulled on his hand toward the doorway which opened into the kitchen. "Oh, hurry, Pop. Hurry. I know exactly what I'm going to wear."

"Don't get your hopes up. We'll change, but only because we have our work clothes on, and we don't want Miss Grace to be embarrassed to ride in the truck with us."

His voice faded as they walked through the kitchen and up the stairs. Haley said something, but Grace didn't catch what it was, or Ches' words as his deeper tone responded to hers.

Grace went into the bathroom and shut the door. Her eyes widened. There was a claw foot tub in the corner. Grace went over to it, and touched the curved edge. Beyond it was a bay window looking out on a tiny shuttered patio. Obviously, it was this way so a person could bathe without worrying someone would see him.

Her.

Whoever.

Not that Grace was thinking of anyone in particular. Men didn't take baths, did they? They took showers instead. But the tub was huge. Grace herself could sit in the tub and stretch her legs out to take a bath. How wonderful that would be. She hadn't been able to straighten her legs in a tub since adolescence. She'd love to take a bath in it.

Grace shook her head.

This was silly. Ches was a nice man. Very nice. But he was also a stranger. A good Samaritan, yes. Grace couldn't finagle using his bathroom to luxuriate in the tub though she doubted he would mind. It seemed he was willing to put aside his evening plans to help a woman in distress, and even attend a wedding just because his little girl wanted to.

Where was Haley's mother? Not that it was any of Grace's business.

She unzipped the skirt and slid it down her legs, then stepped out of it. Quickly, she put on the pants. Obviously, his. They practically swallowed her. Opening the door, she walked to the dryer and opened it. Was it okay to go ahead and put her skirt in? She peered in the opening. It was empty. Placing the clothing inside, she studied the panel, turned a knob, then pushed a button. The machine started.

Now what?

She should have felt more uncomfortable being in a stranger's house, wearing his clothes, using his dryer, but she didn't. It felt good somehow, like she had come up on a surprise, a pearl in an old shell found on the beach.

She hugged herself and smiled. What would people think if they knew she had accepted a ride from someone she didn't know, that she'd willingly come into his house. Of course, if little Haley hadn't been around, Grace probably wouldn't feel as secure. But the child acted as a great chaperone, even if she didn't realize it. And it was clear that she had Ches wrapped around her little finger.

Grace opened the bathroom door and shock ran through her. A large gray dog stood in the laundry room and studied her.

"Hello." She held her hand out so he could sniff it. "You must be Jojo."

He sniffed opening his jaws, revealing a big pink tongue now hanging from his massive mouth. He stepped toward her and pushed his head into her hand.

"Aren't you a big boy?" she said to him patting him and scratching behind his ears.

In a few minutes, thunder sounded through the house. Jojo looked back and turning, walked out of the room. Grace surmised the noise was the sound of footsteps running down stairs because Haley came through the kitchen wearing a blue princess dress complete with tiara. She had a wand in her hand.

"Hi! I'm ready."

Grace blinked at her. "What a beautiful dress."

Haley held out the skirt and twirled around. "I do have a bride dress, but Pop said it's bad manners to wear white to the wedding unless you're the bride, and you definitely can't wear a bride dress because then it will get fusing."

"Confusing, I bet was what he meant."

"Yeah. Confusing." Haley pursed her lips as she looked at her hands. "I wish I had some lady gloves. I wanted to wear Pop's gloves, but he gots a hole in 'em because they got caught on the bobbed wire, and he said they're too dirty and big for me anyway. So, how long till your skirt's dry?"

Surprised at the girl's sudden silence as she waited for an answer to her question, Grace shrugged. "I don't know. Maybe twenty minutes."

"We won't be late, will we?"

"Maybe a little."

"Aww, gee. I hate to be late. I want to see the bride walk down the aisle."

"Yes. That's a pretty important part of the ceremony."

"You ever been to a wedding?"

"A few."

"I've seen some on T.V. but I'd really like to see one for real." Haley reached up and took Grace's hand. "Come on. Let's sit in the den until your skirt gets dry."

She led her through the kitchen into a great room with leather furniture and a massive television on one wall. Little girl toys were scattered all over the floor, and a small vanity was set up in one corner. Haley stopped at the couch. "You sit here, and I'm going to put on some make-up."

"You wear make-up?"

"It's little girl make-up, so I'm allowed."

"Don't put on too much. If you make yourself too pretty, everyone is going to be looking at you and not pay any attention to the bride."

Haley nodded. "Pop says I'm the prettiest girl he knows. I was going to marry him, but he said we're already family, and you marry someone because they ain't family, but you want them to be."

"That's a good way of looking at it."

Booted footfalls alerted Grace that Ches was descending the staircase. She turned and looked up, and nearly lost her breath. Ches wore smoky grey slacks and a dusty pink button-down shirt. He'd changed his boots, too, and their finish shone as if they were new. His smooth jaw testified he'd somehow found time to shave as well. Hatless, now, his dark hair was tinged with silver at the temples. The overall picture caused her heart to flutter, and Grace looked away in case the admiration she felt for his appearance showed on her face.

"Why don't you see if your skirt is dry, Miss Grace. Then we can go to the wedding," Haley suggested.

"Little Bit, I told you that we aren't going to the wedding. We can't invite ourselves that way. We'll take Miss Grace, and you and I will go somewhere close by and wait on her."

"I am allowed to bring one guest," Grace said.

"Just one?" Haley said with a disappointed gaze. "Can it be me?"

"I'm sure it would be fine if you both came."

"Really?" Haley jumped up and down.

"It's just…." Grace shook her head at Ches. "I hate to put you out this way."

"If you don't mind us being there, Sugar, we don't mind going. Little Bit can hardly contain herself, and it gives us a good excuse to get out of the house."

"Yeah. A real good excuse, and we don't mind going one bit."

Grace chuckled. "I believe you."

Haley placed her hands on her hips. "You think your skirt is dry? I don't think sweat pants are going to cut it."

"Indeed," Grace said and went to check on the skirt.

In a few minutes they were back out at the truck. Ches moved Haley's car seat to the middle. "It will give you a little more leg room," he explained.

"And I can talk to both of you a lot easier too," Haley added.

"Always an important thing to consider," Grace said.

They settled into the truck, and Ches backed out of the garage and turned around in the yard on a rock path obviously made for that purpose. He headed south. The drive was punctuated with Haley's monologues, on a variety of subjects from ice cream to movies to Jojo. Soon they were entering the town of Athens City.

"Athens City looks like a nice place," Grace said.

"It is," Ches replied.

"See that? That's where I'm going to go to school next year."

Grace peered at the building.

"It looks a great place to go to school."

"I'll be in kindergarten." The pride of her expression lit up her face.

"Bet your pop is going to miss having you home during the day."

"Naw, he won't 'cause he's too busy growing corn and raising cows. I stay with Miss Aretha during the day, don't I, Pop?"

"Yep."

"Now, she's going to miss me something fierce, don't you think, Pop?"

"Yep."

Grace looked at Ches but couldn't read his expression. He was watching the road. The pink starched sleeve of his shirt ended at his wrist with silver cufflinks. Cufflinks? A lot of trouble to go to just to drive a stranger to a wedding in another town.

"Miss Aretha only lets me watch an hour of televisiom a day cause she says televisiom rots your brains, but there's lots of good kid shows on, and they are educational. I asked Pop to speak to her about it, but he says Miss Aretha gets to be the boss at her house, so he don't get no say."

"Hmm."

"She's the boss at her house cause her husband died. Pop's the boss at our house, ain't you, Pop?"

"Yep."

"If Sissy ever gets her own house, she'll get to be the boss, and she won't have to live by Pop's rules no more. But I ain't going to live with her if I can help it, cause she don't know how to cook. Pop does all the cooking, and all Sunni can do is open a can of Spaghettio's, and they're all right every once in while, but man can't live on Spaghettio's alone, can he, Pop?"

"Nope."

"You like Spaghettio's, Miss Grace?"

"I haven't had them in a long time."

"What's your favorite food?"

"Oh, my. I like lots of things."

Haley kicked her feet a few times as if timing Grace's hesitation.

"I like… chicken casserole."

"Chicken casserole!" The child's tone indicated she didn't approve of Grace's choice. Her feet increased their rhythm. "I can't stand that stuff. All those peas and carrots. No way, man."

"My mom's chicken casserole didn't have peas and carrots in it."

Haley's feet stilled. "No peas and carrots?"

"No."

The truck was quiet except for the hum of the tires on the road.

"Pop, did you know you could make chicken casserole without the peas and carrots?"

"Nope."

She shook her head at him. "I coulda liked it all this time, but you were doing it wrong."

Ches and Grace laughed.

Haley carried the conversation the entire way to Athens City with little more than monosyllabic answers from Ches. Grace told him the name of the church where the wedding was, and he nodded.

"Do you know where it is?"

"Yep."

Yep. Nope. The man's repertoire of words wasn't very impressive, even if he did look good cleaned up, and he was in the small percentage of men taller than she was.

When Ches' truck arrived at the church, the parking lot

was full, and the bride was standing outside of the front door which elicited a squeal of excitement from Haley. Ches pulled up past the building and parked on the curb. Quickly, he unbuckled Haley and put her on his hip as she urged him to hurry. Grace began to walk toward the church with trepidation.

Haley whined from behind her. Yeah, Grace could relate.

She hated being late.

She'd just have to wait until Denise walked most of the way down the aisle, then she'd slip in the back.

"Little Bit," Ches said softly.

Grace paused and glanced behind her. Ches and Haley were looking at each other solemnly.

"You have to be quiet. Do you understand?"

Her lip quivered a little.

Grace pivoted, walked back to them, and tugged at the girl's pigtail.

"Do you know whose day is this?" she asked the little girl.

She shook her head.

"This is Lord's day," Grace said. "And the bride and groom want the Lord to bless them in it. That's why they came here to the church to get married. We don't want to mess it up for them by being upset. It's a happy day."

"A happy day." Haley sighed. "Okay." She straightened a bit.

"So, we're going to button our lips," Ches added. "And we aren't going to make a peep once we get in there, so if you have to go potty, you better just tell me now so we can go and not miss anything."

"No way. I don't have to potty, and I'll button my lip."

"Good girl." He leaned into her and kissed her forehead.

My gosh, he's a good parent. Grace wondered what happened to his wife. Haley had said he'd said he was too set in his ways to get married. Did that mean he never had been married? Oh, what's it matter? He's just a good

Samaritan who would obviously drive a stranger to a wedding just because his little girl wanted to go. He probably had a line of women who would go out with him if he snapped his fingers. Grace shook her head and picked up her pace toward the church.

She felt skin against her hand, then Ches' hand enveloped hers and he tugged her toward the side of the building. She looked up at him.

"Side door," he said with a nod of his head. "Let's try it."

Sure enough, down the sidewalk he was currently leading them to, a side door was propped open. When Grace looked in the doorway, she saw it opened near the front of the sanctuary, and warm humid air met her. Everyone inside was standing. Obviously, Denise had begun her entrance. A man in a suit smiled at Denise and handed her a funeral fan.

"Sorry. The air conditioning isn't working." He pointed them to an empty spot on a pew about two-thirds of the way back.

Grace walked down the side aisle discreetly. Ches had dropped her hand when they entered the church, but her fingers still tingled from the contact. His grasp had been firm, his skin calloused.

Working man's hands.

She often held the hands of a patient at the hospital, but that was while she was working. It was her job—to offer comfort, to ease suffering, to lend aid—all of those things that a chaplain did in her daily routine. She knew that human touch could be healing to someone sick. She had experienced that herself when she had been ill.

But it had been a long time—a very long time—since she'd held the hand of a man outside of her job.

And it felt very nice.

Grace slipped into a pew, and Ches followed her. Denise was nearly to the front now. Grace noted that Denise's dad wasn't walking her down the aisle this time. He'd done that for her first wedding, and maybe they felt since he'd given her away to Jim already, she was on her own to walk down this aisle.

Grace smiled at the thought, hoping it wasn't too catty.

She looked at her companions, and saw Haley straining to see Denise. But Ches was watching her, his eyebrows raised, and his mouth turned up on one side. He was hoping Haley was going to be able to keep her promise about being quiet. Grace felt she was in on the conspiratorial secret. She didn't care whether Haley made a fuss or not. There were enough children in the extended family that the chances of some kid making noise was pretty good, especially as warm as it was in here.

In less than half an hour the ceremony was over.

She met Ches' eyes and nodded toward the door where they'd entered. He headed that way while most everyone followed the wedding party out of the main entrance. Grace breathed a sigh when they got outside from the oppressive heat of the sanctuary.

"Where's the wedding cake?" Haley asked. "They didn't even cut it or dance or anything!"

"That part comes at the reception," Grace said.

The little girl's eyebrows which had been drawn down in righteous indignation rose in intrigue. "The reception," she whispered in wonder. She turned and looked upward at her pop bringing Grace's attention to him as well.

His gaze was on Grace, a twinkle in his eye. "Were you going?"

A self-deprecating smile lifted her lips. She hadn't really planned to.

"Well, of course, she was, Pop. Come on."

He smiled because he knew the truth. "I see," he said to Haley, but the response was really Grace's.

"We should go," Grace said.

"If you want to."

"Why would she come all this way and nearly get killed by a deer, just to miss the cake and dancing? Pop, what planet are you living on?"

"Indeed," Grace declared.

People walked past them to a building adjacent to the sanctuary. Aunt Margaret, Denise's mother, approached and paused. "Well, Grace." The older woman stepped up and embraced her. "You did make it. How wonderful." Releasing her, she noticed the man and girl with Grace, and gave them an inquiring glance before turning to Grace.

"Aunt Margaret, this is Ches and Haley. This is my Aunt Margaret and mother of the bride."

"How do you do?"

"Miss Grace was allowed to bring a guest, and she said you probably wouldn't mind if she brought two, since I'm a little kid and all. I don't eat a lot."

Margaret bent down to meet the gaze of the child. "You eat as much as you want. Come on. You can go with me to the fellowship hall, and we'll see if we can get some punch. The heat in that church made me thirsty." She held out her hand, and Haley clasped it. They walked on the sidewalk leading to the door of the building.

Ches stared after them. "So, she's your aunt. Are you two very close?"

"Not now, though we used to be when I was young. She loves children, as you can tell."

"Little Bit is painfully shy." He cut his eyes to Grace. "At some point, she really needs to come out of her shell."

Grace laughed. "Your daughter doesn't take after you, does she?"

"She's not my daughter biologically. My sister's child, but I've had her since she was eight months old, so she doesn't know the difference."

"Oh." On the brink of apologizing, Grace didn't. Ches' easy-going manner didn't invite one.

"Sunni's mother has been gone for about nine years now." They followed Margaret and Haley at a more leisurely pace. "So it's just me, Sunni, and Haley."

"What happened to Sunni's mother?"

"Vanessa and I were both very young when we married. High school sweethearts. One day I came in from the field, and there's a deputy on the porch. He served me divorce papers. After the shock wore off, I signed the papers. She took Sunni, but after a couple of years and with a new husband, she decided Sunni would be better off with me." His warm green eyes held no trace of bitterness. "I agree, and Sunni agrees most of the time."

"You're a good dad to both of them, I'm sure."

They arrived at the door of the building, and Ches held the door open for her. As she walked by him, Grace was struck again with how tall he was. As she crossed the threshold, she looked around at the interior of the building decorated with miles of tulle and fairy lights. Round tables covered in white and lavender cloths filled the perimeter of the room, and a band on the far end of the room were already playing to an empty interior which was to be the dance floor.

Several long tables at the back of the room held enough food to feed the crowd of people arriving. At the center was a massively tiered wedding cake. Margaret and Haley stood in front of it, and Haley jumped up and down several times. The child's excited chatter reached them.

"You sure made her night by allowing us to come. She'll be talking about this for months," Ches said.

"You did me the favor by bringing me."

"So, what should we do?"

"Claim a table, I suppose."

Already people were sitting down. "Anyone you want to sit with?"

"Not a lot of our family is here. It's her second marriage, so it's a lot smaller than the first."

She chose a table and they sat. Haley ran to them, a grin across her face. "Miss Margaret says when the bride and groom get here, we can eat, but she let me have swipe of the icing in the back of the groom's cake cause she said no one cares about it, only the bride's cake. And it's chocolate too, which is even better."

Margaret arrived with a cup of punch. She set it down on the table. "Here's Haley's drink. I told her I'd bring it over, as she was afraid she'd spill it."

Ches had stood up when Margaret approached. "Much obliged, Miss Margaret," he intoned.

Margaret gazed at him and smiled. "How long have you and Grace been dating?"

Embarrassment engulfed Grace. Her gaze to flew to Ches, who returned Margaret's smile without a touch of discomfort. His lips opened in a charming grin, "Oh, I'd say, about two hours or so."

Margaret's head tilted. "No. I meant, how long have you been seeing each other?"

"Miss Grace had to put on Pop's pants at the house cause all she had were her big girl panties to wear, and Pop wouldn't let her talk to Jester Mason to get her car out of the ditch cause everybody knows he's a ladies man."

Grace's mouth fell open, first from the picture Haley was painting about Grace and Ches, and then with the new information that Ches may have been withholding information about the tow truck man. When she looked at Ches, his expression gave no indication Haley's monologue had bothered him.

"It's quite a story cause she was almost killed by a deer," Haley concluded.

"It sounds like quite a story." Margaret gave a meaningful look to Grace. "Perhaps I could hear it some other time. Will you excuse me?"

"All right," Haley agreed. "Though I didn't actually see the deer." Haley leaned over the table toward Grace. "Was it a doe or a buck, Miss Grace?"

"Err, I don't know." Heat burned her face and neck. She reached up a hand to touch her warm cheek.

"Did it have horns? That's how you tell." Haley waited for her to answer.

"No. I don't think it had horns."

"A girl then. It was probably being chased by a buck. They were probably—"

"Little Bit," Ches interrupted. Haley leaned over to look at Ches, and he shook his head at her.

She blinked at him. "What?"

He patted the back of the chair next to him. "Sit down here."

"I want to sit between you and Miss Grace."

Ches rose from the chair and stood behind it, bending his head to Haley in invitation. She settled in it, and he pushed her forward.

"Thank you, Pop."

"You're welcome. Look. The bride and groom just came in. See? They're going to cut the cake."

Haley moved to her knees to gain height and a better view. She shot a glance of appeal to her pop.

"Go on. But don't get too close, all right? Remember, this is their day."

"The Lord's day," Haley corrected.

"Fine. Stay out of the way."

"Okay," Haley said and skipped away.

Grace watched the couple cut the cake as the photographer took pictures. Denise, in her wedding dress, smiled at Danny. Even their first names matched. Grace didn't fault her cousin for finding happiness. Her first marriage had ended in a painful divorce after Denise discovered he'd been unfaithful.

She noticed Ches studying her.

"How come?" he asked.

"How come what?"

He indicated the couple. "How come you're not married."

Grace had dated a few boys in high school and college, but nothing had ever worked out. Grace didn't mind being single. She had a few close friends she could go out with if she wanted to, but she liked her life.

She shrugged. "No one ever asked me."

"I didn't realize women waited these days to be asked."

Grace smiled. "Did your ex-wife ask you?"

Ches sat back. "I guess you could say Vanessa's daddy was actually the one who suggested she and I get married. So, we did."

Oh.

"Now, don't jump to any conclusions. Sunni didn't come along until a year later. Vanessa was always very defiant, except with me. We'd been together since she was fourteen, and I was fifteen. Her daddy had about all he could stand, and thought her getting married to me would settle her down once and for all." Ches paused, his eyes crinkled at the corners as his mouth turned up suddenly. "Every time I ask you a question, I end up talking about me. You're good at not talking about yourself, aren't you?"

Grace turned her attention the perfunctory wedding rituals at the reception. The band announced the couple would have their first dance as husband and wife, and Denise and Danny walked hand in hand toward the dance floor.

"Professional habit, I suppose."

"What profession?"

"I work at Regional Hospital."

Ches quirked an eyebrow, but didn't say anything. Yes, he realized she hadn't told him what she did, only where she did it. Haley appeared at the table, leaning against Ches, her attention on the dance floor.

"They have to do the first dance by themselves, then we can dance," she said.

Ches turned his head to watch the couple and placed his arm around the little girl. The love apparent between them caused a lump to form in Grace's throat. Ches looked at her then as if he could sense her watching him and Haley. His mouth turned up at the corner, as if inviting her into the moment. Lifting his other hand, he nudged back the chair next to him, and Grace moved into it. When she did so, Haley wedged her body between the two of them, and it was as if Grace had become part of the image of affection shared between uncle and niece, though those terms didn't do their relationship justice. Ches was like a daddy to that girl. The attachment so strong, Grace felt the warmth of it sitting next to them.

It spread through her chest, like eating tomato soup and grilled cheese sandwiches after playing out in the snow all afternoon.

"You're supposed to be looking at the bride and groom, Miss Grace," Haley said.

"I'm sorry. You're just such a pretty little girl. It's hard not to look at you."

"Good thing I didn't wear white, huh?"

"Wicked good."

Grace's use of the little girl's word from earlier in the evening brought a smile to her face. She reached up and hugged Grace.

"You are such a sweet girl," she said as she returned the embrace.

"You're a good hugger."

"Thank you."

"Pop says hugs make lots of things better."

"I believe that. I get to hug people where I work, and there are times when I see where a hug helps when nothing else does."

A shiver of excitement coursed through Haley's body, and she giggled. "That's why you're good at it then. Because it's your job."

Grace stood. "Am I the only one who is hungry? I think I want to try some of that groom's cake."

"Oooh, great idea," Haley said, then shot off through the crowd toward the tables laden with food.

Ches rose and Grace's eyes involuntarily tracked his motion. She paused then followed the child, Ches' booted steps behind her. Once clear of the tables, he appeared beside her, and once at the buffet table, he called Haley to him, and guided her through the line.

After they sat down and ate, Haley convinced Ches to dance with her. They stood, and to Grace's surprise, Haley took her hand as well.

"Come on," the girl commanded.

Grace looked at her in confusion. "What? I thought you were going to dance with Pop."

Haley gave her a look of exasperation. "We're all going to. Geez."

Grace resisted. "Usually just two people dance at a time."

"Yeah, but I'm a little kid. Pop will break his back if you don't come along to help lift me up if we get crazy out there."

"I've seen him pick you up without any strain."

Haley lifted her arm in indignation. "This is dancing. Come on. You'll see. We need you."

Helplessly, Grace looked at Ches hoping he'd excuse her.

He shrugged his shoulders. "I've found it's better to pick your battles, Miss Grace." He'd paused before he spoke her name, and though he had used the polite Southern title Haley also used with her first name, it caused goosebumps to rise on Grace's skin.

What could she do?

Chapter Three

Grace rose from her chair and allowed the child to pull her out on the dance floor. Her heart hammered against her ribs as she played through what Haley had in mind. All of the scenarios seemed awkward. Not that she would mind being so close to the little girl, but being close to her pop, well, that was a different story.

A feel good tune surrounded them as they arrived on the dance floor. Haley jumped and laughed, and swirled around, her shiny skirt billowing out, then she grasped Ches' hand. "Let's all join hands and make a circle so you can swing me," she instructed. Grace and Ches followed the little girl's direction and held their arms taut as the little girl moved back and forth between them. "Isn't this fun?" she said, her face alight with joy.

Yes, Grace, thought, as the enthusiasm radiated outward from Haley to her. Yes, it really was. When a slower song began, Haley's movements calmed, and she swayed first to the left then to the right against their arms. Relaxing, she leaned back, and it was only the adults who held her arms which kept her from falling to the floor.

"Pop," she sang with the melody. "Pop, Haley, and Grace are dancing, dancing, to the music. What are the real words, Poppy?"

"I don't know," Pop sang in reply.

Grace smiled at his playfulness. When she turned to him, his expression was calm, but he winked at her.

"Miss Grace, what are the real words?" Haley sang.

"It doesn't have words," Grace said.

"You're supposed to sing," Haley counseled.

Grace cleared her throat. "All right. The song has no words tonight."

Haley squealed and, dropping their hands, she launched herself at Grace. Grace gasped in surprise and would have fallen back with the force, but Ches caught Haley against Grace's body, and with his other arm, steadied her.

"You okay?" he asked Grace, then to the girl. "Little Bit, you do that to me, and it's fine because I know to expect it, but Miss Grace doesn't. You could have knocked her down."

"Sorry," she sang. "I just got excited." Her tone nor her gleeful expression reflected any remorse.

They danced with every song, until Haley declared that she had to go to the bathroom. The trio began to walk off the dance floor, when Aunt Margaret appeared.

"Does someone need to use the restroom?" She held out her hand. "I'll take her."

"Oh, that's all right. I can—" Grace began.

"Nope." Margaret shook her head. "This is for couple's only. You two go back there and dance."

Grace watched Aunt Margaret and Haley leave wanting to go with them so she wouldn't make a fool of herself with Ches. Her gaze clipped to his and held because he was watching her.

"Want to get something to drink?" he asked.

Relief blanketed her. "Yes."

He smiled, and they walked toward the table where three crystal bowls containing punch, tea, and water sat on raised daises.

"It's not that I don't want to...." Grace said. But what? She didn't want to. Even thinking about it filled Grace with mortification.

"But you don't want to." Ches shrugged. "It's all right, sugar. You don't have to explain yourself."

"I'm sorry."

Ches stopped and turned to her. "Grace, you can count on me to mean what I say. No need to apologize or say why." He bent his head to her. "It's all right. Truly." His easygoing expression and tone demonstrated he did mean what he said.

Grace nodded, and they walked on, arriving at the table. In silence, they picked up the glass cups of water already poured.

"I would like to tell you," Grace said quietly. "Because I think you would understand."

They stood at the edge of the tables standing side by side as they watched the dancers. "All right."

"When I was thirteen, I was five foot six. I was taller than everyone in my class including my teacher. When I was sixteen, I was six feet tall. No one wants to dance, let alone date, a girl who towers over them. I went to a small school, and we didn't have a girls' basketball team, even though the joke was I was tall enough to be the girls' basketball team."

Ches didn't reply. When Grace found the courage to look at him, his eyes twinkled and he smiled.

"Six feet?" he asked.

"Six one."

He snickered. "Shortie."

Grace smiled. There's a name she'd never been called before.

When Haley joined them, her crestfallen expression met them. "How come you're not dancing?"

"We needed a break. You had us out there almost an hour," Ches said as he picked Haley up and settled her in his arms.

The drummer signaled an attention, and the lead singer spoke. "We'll ask all of the eligible bachelors to gather on the dance floor."

"What are they going to do?" Haley asked.

"There's a tradition where the groom will toss the bride's garter—"

"A what?" Haley asked.

Ches blew a breath out.

"It's sort of like a bracelet for a woman's leg," Grace offered.

"Can I get a garter, Pop?"

"I don't think so. Not until you're married. Maybe not even then."

"Okay, so the groom throws the garter?"

"Yes, to all the single men. Whoever catches it is

supposed to be the next one to get married. Then the bride will throw her bouquet to the single women. The woman who catches it then is to be the next one to be married."

Haley's forehead wrinkled. "You mean the boy and girl who are good catchers have to marry each other?"

"No, although it makes a lot of sense that they should," Ches said.

"Should you go out there, Pop?"

He shook his head. "I already had my turn at marriage. I think it's good to leave it to the not married yet people."

"Can I go catch the bouquet when the girls go out?"

"I suppose you could, but you're too young yet to get married."

"What about Miss Grace?"

Grace grimaced. "I'd rather not, thank you."

"But why not? Don't you want to get married?" Haley asked.

"It's not that I don't want to get married, but competing with other people to catch flowers in the hopes that I would get married seems desperate."

Haley blinked at her. "Huh?"

"Miss Grace thinks fighting over the bouquet isn't ladylike."

"Oh." Haley yawned.

"Perhaps, we should think about leaving. It's getting late."

"No. I want to stay."

"It is late, Little Bit, and Miss Grace has another forty-five-minute drive after we get home."

"If my car is out of the ditch."

"It is. Jester texted me and said your car is parked in front of the house. He checked it over and said there wasn't any damage."

Grace smiled in relief. "Good news."

They left the reception, the warm night enveloping them as they made their way to the truck. As Ches buckled Haley into her car seat, she asked Grace. "Would you come and see us again?"

"I suppose I could."

"Pop's birthday is next week. Maybe you could come be a date for him and we could go out."

Grace searched her mind for an appropriate response, but none came to mind. She was afraid to look at Ches to see his reaction. Thankfully, the interior of the truck was dark. Ches inserted the key in the ignition and started the engine. The lights on the dashboard glowed.

Finally, Grace spoke. "That's kind of you to invite me, Haley, but I'm sure Pop already has plans for his birthday."

"No, he doesn't. Do you, Pop?"

"No, Little Bit, but if Miss Grace comes over for a date on my birthday, you'll have to stay with Miss Aretha."

"I can't go on the date?"

"Not my birthday date."

"But I won't get to see Miss Grace."

"Sure you will. She'll come to the house, then we'll take you to Miss Aretha's before the date."

"Why can't I go?"

"Because it will be a date. You're not old enough to date."

"I go on play dates."

"Yeah, but this is an adult date. No playing involved. Just boring stuff, like dinner, and what else, Grace?"

"Umm." Thoughts swirled in Grace's head. She hadn't actually been asked, but it seemed as if the date was a done deal. What would be boring for Haley? "A lecture on paint drying?"

Ches laughed.

"What's a lecture?"

"Somebody talking," Grace said.

"Somebody talking about paint drying?" Haley asked in disbelief. "Who talks about that?"

"Boring people. Boring adult people," Ches answered.

Haley didn't reply, and soon Grace suspected she had fallen asleep. Contentment settled on Grace. She watched the road illuminated by the headlights.

After a while, Ches spoke. "Are you awake?"

"Yes, but I don't think Haley is."

"No. She usually falls asleep on a trip especially when it's dark."

"I can remember sleeping in the car on the way home from seeing my grandparents. They lived in the country, and we'd go up there on Sundays and stay until dark." Grace sighed at the memory. "The stars in the sky back then look a lot like the stars tonight."

"You grew up in the city?"

"Yes. That's why it was such a treat to go to Meemee's. So much space to explore and run around. Good memories. What about you? Did you grow up here?"

"No. I'm a city boy, too, if you can believe it."

"How did you end up farming?"

Ches smiled. "I, too, had family who lived in the country. Used to beg to go to the farm on the weekends when I was little. Some of my best memories as a kid was working in the fields with my Uncle Bill who lived with my grandma. When my uncle died, my grandma still lived out here by herself. Shortly after Sunni was born, she went to live at a retirement home. She gave me the deed to the farm so we moved out here. Vanessa hated it. Said it was too far from town, and she...." He blew out a breath.

"She what?"

"Sugar, I don't know what it is that makes me talk so much around you."

"Perhaps working on a farm doesn't give you the chance to talk to other people," Grace said.

"No, what is it about you?"

"Oh." Good question. "Most of your interaction is probably with Haley, and her questions are from a five-year-old's perspective."

"Did you have cousins you played with at your grandparents' house?"

"Oh, yes. My mother had seven brothers and sisters, and all of their kids would be there. I was an only child, and it was lonely. I loved having so many children to play with. Were there many cousins when you would go see your grandparents?"

"No cousins. Just my sister. Did your grandparents have a working farm?"

Grace answered, realizing Ches was deliberately keeping the topic on her. "How come you don't want to talk about yourself?" she asked.

"How come you don't?"

Grace smiled. Touché. "I'm not used to it."

"Neither am I. Not that I mind, but I'd like to know about you. I already know about me."

"We could trade facts about ourselves. Share some things most people don't know."

"All right. You go first."

"I'm allergic to bananas. They make my inner ears itch."

Ches low laughter filled the cab. "Hard to scratch there."

"No kidding."

"Let's see. Huh. Something no one else knows. When I was twelve, I found a snakeskin and I put it on the back porch of Mrs. Simmons, our neighbor who always yelled at the neighborhood kids for walking through her yard."

"Oh, dear. The worst thing like that I probably ever did was I was playing with matches one time, and set our storage house on fire. Got in big trouble for it, too. But no one was hurt."

"I've got one. It's kind of a downer though," Ches said. In the quiet of the truck cab, his low voice flowed soothingly over her.

"Tell me. I can handle it."

"My mother drowned in a boating accident when I was a kid. She'd given us a beach ball to play with, and for the first several months after her death, I would suck in a little air from the ball before I'd go to sleep at night because she had blown up the ball the morning she died, and it made me feel closer to her because it was her breath I was breathing in."

Tears collected in Grace's eyes. "It is a downer. But it's

also a very sad and sweet story."

"No one knew about the ball, and after the air was gone, it made it extra hard because it was like there was nothing left of her for me to have."

Grace reached her hand and touched his resting on the steering wheel. He squeezed her fingers.

When they arrived at the house, Grace's car was parked to the side of the driveway. Ches drove by it, the garage door opening. He turned off the engine and removed Haley, still asleep, from her seat. His eyes met hers over Haley's head. "I'm going to put her to bed."

Unsure what he expected of her, Grace followed him inside. Though she couldn't have weighed much, he strode with the child across the room and up the stairs. Grace shifted from one foot to the other.

"Grace?" Ches called to her. "Would you come up here? Second door on the left."

Curiously, Grace did as he asked. The second door on the left was obviously Haley's bedroom. Ches stood next to the bed. "She woke up and wants to say good night to you."

"I thought you had already left," Haley said in a sleepy voice.

Grace approached the bed. "Good night, sweet girl."

Haley lifted her arms in an invitation for a hug. Grace bent forward and hugged her. When Grace would have straightened, Haley's arms tightened. "Don't go, Miss Grace."

Grace patted her, then sat down on the bed, and Haley dropped her arms, but grasped Grace's hand. "Why don't we say a goodnight prayer? That will help you get back to sleep."

Haley nodded.

"Do you want to say one, or do you want me to?"

"You. But not the Now I lay me down to sleep one. I don't want the Lord to take my soul."

Understanding warmed Grace's heart. Losing her mother when she was so young perhaps made her worry about such things. "Okay. Close your eyes." Grace closed her own eyes and bowed her head. "Lord, I have passed another day, and come to thank Thee for Thy care. Forgive my faults in work or play, and listen to my evening prayer. Thy favor gives me daily bread, and friends, who all my wants supply: and safely now I rest my head, preserved and guarded by Thine eye. Amen." Opening her eyes, she looked at the little girl. "I'm glad I met you," she said to her.

Haley smiled a sleepy smile, and turned to her side. "Me too," she sighed and closed her eyes.

Grace watched her for a moment before she stood. She noticed Ches there still in the room leaning against the wall with his arms crossed. She nodded at him and walked to the door and down the stairs. His footsteps echoed behind her in the quiet house. The living room, lit only by a corner lamp, complimented the ambient peace of the prayer upstairs. She turned around to face him.

"I really appreciate everything you did today."

"My pleasure."

Attraction pulled at Grace. She acknowledged the feeling, appreciated the height and breadth of this man, the hue of his eyes, the kind curve of his mouth, the tenderness of a bond between him and Haley, and the generosity of giving up his evening to help out a stranded woman on the side of the road.

"I'm glad I met you," she said using the same words she'd uttered to Haley. And meaning them this time as well.

Ches smiled. "Me too."

"When is your birthday?"

"A week from today. I didn't want to celebrate it, to be honest. I'm surprised Little Bit remembered."

Grace decided he wasn't going to issue an invitation for the date. Disappointment began to edge into her throat. "Children still think birthdays are worth celebrating."

"Would you like to come down next Saturday, or are you busy?"

Grace took a few deep breaths attempting to slow the

pace of her heart. "I'm not busy. What time?"

"Oh, maybe six? I could meet you in Carlton, but Little Bit wouldn't get to see you."

"I can be at your house at six." Happiness spread through her chest. "Ches?"

"Yes, sugar?"

"Do you know where there are any paint-drying lectures on a Saturday night?"

He chuckled. "I'll go by the hardware store this week and find out."

****

Grace's mother texted her Tuesday with a directive to call when she had a few minutes to chat. Grace looked at the small screen, smiling. Aunt Margaret must have talked to mom and told her about the guests Grace had brought with her to the wedding. She scrolled through her contacts and pressed the icon to call.

"Hello," her mother answered.

"Hi, Mom."

"Shall we chit chat first, or will you just go ahead and tell me who you were with at Denice's wedding?" Penny, her mother, said.

Grace smiled. She liked this about her mom. Honest and upfront. "I'd like to tell you there's something to it, but the truth is, I had a little mishap on my way down there. A very nice man helped me out and accompanied me to the wedding." She shrugged.

"A mishap?" Her mother's skeptical tone invited further explanation.

"A deer ran out in front of my car. I swerved to miss it and ended up in a ditch. Ches came along and helped me out."

"And brought you to the wedding with his little girl?"

"Haley is his niece actually. Super nice people, Mom. You'd love them."

"Really? That's all there was to it? What man helps a woman with her car in the ditch by taking her to a wedding?"

"Haley, his little niece really wanted to come to the wedding. She'd never been to one before, and I suppose they had nothing better to do."

Penny didn't reply.

"Mom?"

"Margaret said you and he acted like you knew each other very well. She said you told her you and he were dating."

Grace laughed. "Oh, Mom. She asked us how long we had been dating, and Ches said a few hours. He was just making a joke."

"Oh." The short word contained a world of disappointment. "Well. All right then." By the time she got to *All right then*, some cheerfulness had returned.

Poor Mom. Though she'd never harassed Grace about having a boyfriend or getting married, she knew her mom worried Grace was alone.

"Don't get too excited, but I'm actually going out on a date with him Saturday."

"Oh, Grace, really?"

Too late not to get excited apparently if Penny's enthusiasm was any indication.

"Mom, it's just a date. Haley actually cornered him about asking me out. He was probably just being nice, but I'm looking forward to it."

"You'll let me know, won't you, how it goes?"

"Sure, Mom. But, you know, it's no big deal. He was just being nice."

"Margaret said he's very tall. And very handsome."

"He is tall."

"And handsome?"

"I…suppose so."

"I wish I had called you with video chat on your phone. That way I could look at your face and tell if you think he's handsome."

"He is. Really handsome, all right?"

"And you'll call me and tell me how the date went?"

Grace blew out a breath of exasperation. "Yes, but it's

probably just a one-time thing, so don't be doing any wedding planning of your own, please?"

****

Grace should have called first.

She stood on the front porch dressed in her prettiest blouse, frilly with tiny buttons down the front, and soft knit pants. She'd washed her hair this afternoon, styling it, and leaving it loose about her shoulders. She'd even dabbed perfume on her pulse points and behind her ears. This was a date, after all. An adult date. At least, it was supposed to be.

She shifted to her other hand the bag she held with two gift wrapped presents inside: one for Ches and one for Haley. Reaching forward, Grace knocked on the door since depressing the doorbell had neglected to bring anyone to her summons.

Another minute passed.

No one was home.

Disappointment blanketed her. Did she have the day wrong? They had said Saturday, right? She reached into her purse and pulled out her cell phone. Looking at the screen, she sighed.

No signal.

Had Ches forgotten, or had he remembered and decided not to be at the house when she arrived?

Silly. She was silly for getting excited about a date. Ches probably had a girlfriend already, and didn't know how to get out of going on the date with Grace.

She should have called, given him the chance to say he was sick, or busy, or changed his mind. With one last disappointed look at the door, she stepped off the porch to the walkway and her car. She didn't leave the gift. Didn't want proof that she had stood out here like an idiot with gifts. Entering her car, she placed the gift bag on the seat next to her. Driving a few miles, she checked for a signal on her phone, and four miles out, she saw the bars on the screen. Attempting to call Ches, she only got his voice mail. She hung up without leaving a message, but noticed she herself had two missed calls and a voice mail. Pressing the icon, disappointment reigned again.

Neither were from Ches.

One was from the hospital where she worked, and another was from Roman, one of her co-workers. Grace listened to the message.

"Hi, Grace, it's Roman. Sorry to bother you, but something has come up with... a friend, and I need to leave. I'm going to stick it out here at the hospital until midnight, but wondering if you can take night call. Let me know."

The hospital had a chaplain in-house from 8 in the morning until midnight. After that, a chaplain carried a pager and was available to come in if needed.

Grace pressed the icon to return the call. "Hi Roman. I just received your message. Did you find anyone to take your on-call tonight?"

"Not yet. We had a trauma, and I've been too busy to call anyone else."

"I'll take it. As a matter of fact, if you want me to, I'll come in now."

"Really? Are you sure? This is your day off."

"I don't mind. I didn't have anything else to do."

Well, she thought she had, but it turned out she was wrong. Grace opened the glove compartment and picked up her pager. Turning it on, she clipped it to the waistband of her pants, then picked up her chaplain badge setting it on the front of her shirt.

Nothing better for a pity party than visiting patients at the hospital. Most of them were having much worse days then being stood up on a date.

When Grace arrived at Regional Hospital, she called Roman who met her in the office. "Thanks so much for coming in. There was a car wreck on Hwy 40 in Sand Stern, and we had two traumas from it. One a little girl. The family is here, and I just took them up to the patient room, so we're good there. I've been sitting with another family in the surgery waiting room. Their dad had a heart attack, and he's in surgery right now. They're pretty torn up."

Grace nodded. That would be her first visit. As was the practice of the chaplains as they passed the baton of their duties, the leaving chaplain prayed.

Bowing their heads, Roman spoke. "Loving Father, thank you for Grace and the work she will do while she is here. Surround all of us completely in your love and care. May your healing of body and spirit be done in this place. Amen."

"And Lord, help Roman and his friend. Amen," Grace said, not wanting to pry but deciding God's help was surely needed.

"Thanks. Keep praying, would you? My friend's name is Neveah, and she's really troubled." He handed her the hospital phone the chaplain carried while on duty.

"What's the name of the patient in surgery?" Grace asked as Roman was about to walk out the door.

"Last name is Larson. You can't miss the family—a teenager and little girl. They're the only ones in the waiting room."

Grace rode the elevator to the second floor where the surgeries took place and walked toward the large waiting room. On a Saturday, the guest services desk was vacant, and a divider gave family members privacy as they waited for their loved ones to come out of surgery. A cartoon played on the wall-mounted television. She prayed a silent prayer for guidance and stepped around the divider.

A teenage girl in blue jeans and a black T-shirt and dyed black hair sat on the chair with a younger girl lying across another chair with her head in her lap. The little girl had her thumb in her mouth. Though her head was turned toward the television, her gaze was vacant.

Grace's heart thumped in her chest as she studied the scene and recognized the younger of the girls.

"Hi, I'm Grace. I'm a chaplain here. Haley?"

Haley rose and blinked at her. "Miss Grace?" Her eyes filled with tears. "Miss Grace, Pop is bad off."

Chapter Four

Grace sat down and gathered her in her arms patting her on the back. Over her head, Grace sought and captured Sunni's guarded gaze.

"Haley and I met last week. I had some car trouble and she and your dad helped me out."

Sunni shook her head. "I don't understand. What are you doing here?"

"I work here. Roman, the other chaplain, had to go, but he told me you were here, so I wanted to check on you. How long has your dad been in surgery?"

"A couple of hours."

"What happened?"

Sunni began to cry. "It's my fault. It's because of me he's here. What are we going to do if he dies?"

Haley's weeping became louder. Grace moved closer to the young woman. "Sunni, Sunni. Listen to me. This is a good hospital. Good care. If your dad can be helped, he will get that help here. Now take some deep breaths. Breathe with me." Grace exaggerated her breathing to demonstrate. "In and out. That's good. Haley, you too. Breathe in. Breathe out. Another one, in and out. Better?"

Sunni nodded, though tears still spilled from her eyes.

"Good. Did you bring him here?"

"No. They flew him in a helicopter."

"Were you there when it happened?"

"Yes. I heard something crash in the kitchen. When I went in there, he was," Her voice broke. "unconscious on the floor. I tried to wake him up, but he wouldn't come to at first, then he was all confused. I didn't know what to do. I called 911, and he got mad because he said he wasn't going to the hospital. But when they came, he went with them anyway. They said we should come here. By the time we got here, he was already back there. We haven't even seen him yet."

"They said they had to take him right back in surgery.

They said they'd let us know when he was in recovery."

"Well, okay. That sounds hopeful. Don't you think so?"

"Umm. I don't know." Fresh tears leaked from her eyes. "They made me sign these papers, like I know what's going on. He takes care of that stuff. Not me."

"You're his closest relative, and you're an adult, right? You're nineteen?"

"Well." She gulped a breath. "Yeah, but..." She shook her head. "I don't want to be an adult about this."

Grace nodded. "I know. You're scared because he's your dad and you love him. Let me go back there and see what I can find out, okay?"

"All right."

Grace nudged Haley away from her and would have set her down on the chair next to her, but the little girl held tightly to her. "No. No, Miss Grace. No, don't leave us."

"I'm going to check on your pop. Don't you want to know if he's out of surgery?"

Her big green gaze, luminous with unshed tears tore a hole in Grace's heart.

"Do you remember what I told you about hugging people at my work? I said a hug helps when nothing else does."

Haley nodded.

"Come here, then. Let me hug you really, really good for a few minutes. Then I'm going to check on Pop. All right?"

After a while, the little girl relaxed enough, and Grace walked to the secured surgical unit, swiping her badge to open the locked door. No one was at the nurse's station, not surprising since it was the weekend, and all beds were vacant. Grace walked through the pre-surgery area to the post-operation and recovery unit. A man in scrubs sat behind the desk.

He looked up when Grace approached. "May I help you?"

"I'm Grace, the chaplain. I wanted to check on

Chesapeake Larson. Is he out of surgery yet?"

"Not yet."

"Do you know what happened?"

"They took him to the cath lab to place some stents, but his blood pressure dropped, so Dr. Akeem wanted to take extra precautions just in case something happened."

"He'll be in ICU."

"Yep."

"Vented?"

"Shouldn't be once he's through the surgery."

"Would you call me when he is in recovery? I'd like to bring his daughters back to see him." Grace handed the man a card with her telephone extension on it. He nodded and set it on the desk. "Thank you."

Grace walked down the hall and back into pre-surgery. She spied a chair in one of the curtained bays and sat down. Taking a deep breath, then another one, she clinched and unclenched her hands.

Oh, Lord, please let Ches be okay. Those girls really need him.

In a couple of minutes, Grace collected herself enough to go into the lobby and meet Sunni and Haley.

She smiled reassuringly at them as she approached. "He's still in surgery, but they are going to call me when he's finished. Have you all had supper yet?"

They shook their heads.

"Let's go down to the cafeteria and eat. I'm hungry. What about you?"

"Okay," Haley said.

"Sunni?"

She cast a glance over the divider at the door. "I don't know. Are you sure they'll call you?"

"Yes."

Sunni reached down and picked up Haley. "I guess so. If you're sure they will call you."

"They will."

****

As promised the nurse called Grace, and she and the girls went back to the waiting room. Grace went by herself to the recovery unit first, stopping by the nurse's station, but the nurse wasn't there. When Grace looked around the corner to the open room lined with beds, she saw the nurse next to the only occupied bed in the unit. Stepping back and leaning against the wall, she felt her heart hammering in her chest.

Breathe. In and out. Just like you told Sunni and Haley. You can do this.

She lifted her hand to her chest, willing herself to be calm.

Be still. Be still, and know I am God.

The verse drifted into her mind. Grace focused on the message of the Psalm.

Breathe. Breathe. Breathe.

Footsteps approached, and the nurse appeared. "The family can come back. No more than two people though."

"Two is all there is. One's a child, but I'd really like her to see him before he goes upstairs to Intensive Care."

He pursed his lips. "If she's disruptive…"

"I will stay close and monitor her, and escort her out if need be."

He nodded. "And the patient is to lie flat. Not sitting up, not even moving his head off the bed."

Grace nodded in acknowledgement. This was standard in a patient who had undergone a heart cath.

"I will speak to him first before I get his family."

Ches was on the far side of the room, covered in a white sheet to his gown-clad shoulders. His eyes were open, and he stared at the ceiling. Relief and trepidation wrestled in her throat and chest as she approached the bed.

"Hey," she whispered, then cleared her throat. "Do you know who I am?"

He studied her for a few seconds. "Yes, sugar. I know who you are." He began to lift his head.

"No. No. You have to lie flat."

He let his head drop, his gaze on the ceiling.

"How are you feeling?"

He blinked as if still acclimating himself to being here.

Jennifer Johnson

"Did you ever have one of those days?"

Tears smarted behind her eyes at the first words she'd ever said to him. "I have them all the time," she whispered.

He gazed at her. "Did you operate on me?"

Grace's breath caught. Maybe he didn't remember her after all. "No. I'm not the doctor. I'm a chaplain here. Grace. Remember? You rescued me last week, and we went to the wedding."

"You wouldn't tell me what you did. Only that you worked at the hospital. I thought you were a doctor."

Grace shook her head. "I was afraid you'd be uncomfortable if you knew what I did."

"Did it matter?"

"Yes."

"Why?"

"Because some people think they can't be themselves around me."

He sighed. "You shouldn't have come. I can take care of myself." He raised his hand to his head, noticed the IV needle taped to his skin and lowered it. "In spite of...the evidence to the contrary."

"I'm glad I'm here to help you. I owe you."

"You don't owe me anything, sugar."

"Yes, I do. You and Haley helped me that night. You rescued me on the side of the road, then you gave me two wonderful people to go to the wedding with. I was dreading going alone, but it was so nice to have someone with me." The words were inadequate to explain the gratitude she felt toward this gentle man or the special evening she had spent with him and his niece. "So nice to have someone real to be with."

"You usually go out with imaginary people?"

Grace snickered. "I usually stay in with them."

"You're a chaplain."

"Yes."

"Did you pray over me tonight?"

"I haven't stopped since I found out it was you back here."

He smiled and lifted his hand, seeking hers. "Thank you, sugar."

Grace took the hand he offered. "You're welcome. Haley and Sunni are in the waiting room. If you feel up for a visit, I think it would be a good idea. When you leave here, you are going to ICU, and they won't let Haley come back and see you because she's too young. This will be the only time."

"I want to see her, yes."

"And Sunni too?"

Ches shut his eyes briefly, and a brief expression of pain crossed his features. Grace watched him closely, then glanced at the monitor measuring his vitals.

"She doesn't have to come back here. Not if you don't want her to."

Ches' fingers tightened on hers. "She needs to see me. She's going to have to take care of Little Bit until I can get out of here." His heart rate had increased while he spoke, and a line cut deep between his eyebrows. "It's time Sunni—"

"Ches. Chesapeake, Listen to me," she said in a firm but low voice. "Little Bit is going to be fine, just fine. I'll make sure of it. Whatever happened between you and Sunni, put it aside tonight. Your heart needs you to. Little Bit needs you to."

He took a deep breath, the irises of his eyes burning emerald green.

"She's so young."

"They both are. If I have to, I'll take them home with me."

"Jojo."

"Stop it. I will make sure everyone who depends on you is taken care of while you're here."

"Is that your job as a chaplain?"

"No. My job as a chaplain is to lessen your anxiety so you can get better. But since you helped me out the other night, let me help you tonight. Will you let me do that?"

He didn't speak for about thirty seconds. She squeezed

his fingers. "I know it's hard to do."

"I'm not used to it."

"I know, but I can help. Will you let me?"

His mouth tightened, but he nodded in affirmation.

"Are you ready to see your girls?"

"Yes."

Grace moved their entwined fingers back to the bed, released her hold and patted his hand. "It will be all right."

The dejection in his eyes told Grace he didn't believe her.

Grace returned a few minutes later with Haley on her hip and Sunni trailing behind her. Ches gave them a tired smile.

"Pop. Poppy," Haley said brokenly.

"Hey, Little Bit. I'm all right now, so don't be upset."

"I want to hug you."

"He can't hug you right now, sweetie," Grace said. "He has to be still until in the morning."

"Everything went just fine, and as soon as I can, I'll be home."

Grace noticed he hadn't looked at Sunni yet. Grace turned to her, and saw the set expression on her face.

"When can you come home?" Haley whined.

"I don't know yet. Maybe a few days."

"I don't want to go home by myself." Haley started to cry, and Grace patted her back.

"Don't be dumb, Haley. I'll be there too," Sunni snapped.

"Little Bit? Give Pop a kiss." Ches lifted his arms, and Grace carefully lowered her so she could kiss his cheek. "Love you, baby. Grace, take her outside, will you?" Haley laid her head on Grace's shoulder, her thumb back in her mouth.

Grace left Ches' bedside and paused where the nurse stood at the threshold of the unit. They exchanged a meaningful look before Grace stepped around him toward the waiting room.

The nurse would watch out for Ches. If things got too

heated between father and daughter, the nurse would intervene and escort Sunni out.

Grace trusted him to care for his patient, so she left knowing Ches was in good hands.

The nurse's hands and the Lord's hands.

When Sunni appeared a few minutes later, her mouth was set in an angry line, Grace wondered if the nurse had kicked her out or if she had left on her own.

She approached the chairs where they sat. Sunni reached for Haley. "Come on. Let's go home."

"No," the little girl said. "I want to stay with Miss Grace." To emphasize her point, she wrapped her arms around Grace's waist.

Sunni straightened. "Well, you can't because she has to stay here and work." Sunni cut her eyes to Grace before looking at Haley again. "Dad said you had to."

"I don't want to," she said belligerently.

"Haley, what about Jojo?" Grace said. "Don't you think you should go home and check on him? He's probably worried about Pop too."

"Oh, Jojo." Haley dropped her arms and stood. "Sissy, we have to go check on poor Jojo."

Grace stood as well. "Will you all be okay out there?" Grace wanted to go with them, but she'd have to find someone to cover the hospital. Obviously, Roman wouldn't be able to do it, since she had taken his shift.

Sunni's gaze roved over Grace as if she wondered what business it was of hers. "We'll be fine."

Grace reached into her pocket and withdrew a hospital card with the chaplain's extension on it. She wrote her cell number on the front. "If you need me, call me. I'm on call tonight, so if it's after midnight, call the pager."

Sunni took the card but didn't look at it. "What can you do?"

"I have a two bedroom house less than a mile from here. Dogs and children are welcome."

Sunni snorted. "Sure." The word rent with sarcasm.

"Or, if you are wondering how Ches is, call me, and I

can check on him."

"At two in the morning?" A Machiavellian smile covered her face.

"Or three. That's why I have a pager."

The young woman arched an eyebrow. Reaching down, she took Haley's hand. "Come on, Little Bit. Let's go home."

Grace watched them go. Haley turned and waved at her before they walked into the elevator and the doors shut.

In her office later, Grace checked the census on her computer. Her eyes scanned the list of patients in the Intensive Care Unit.

There he was.

Chesapeake Larson, room 410.

Was he there yet?

Uneasiness settled on Grace. This was a conflict of interest, wasn't it? Ches was a patient here, but she had a personal interest in him. They'd had a date tonight. Now she had access to his medical records. Was it appropriate for her to look at his personal information? What was the ethical thing to do? Grace closed her eyes.

Okay. Think. If this were not Ches. If this were any other patient you had visited post-surgery, what would you do?

I would visit him one more time tonight after he arrived in ICU. I would check in with his nurse. If he were asleep, I would pray at his bedside. If he were awake, I would make sure he wasn't too anxious or scared.

Grace went up to the Intensive Care Unit. When she came to the threshold of Ches' room, the curtain was closed all the way, and the light was on. Bending, Grace noticed the nurse's shoes were at the bedside.

She had to treat Ches as any other patient while she was working. Otherwise, it wouldn't be ethical.

Yearning to go in the room nearly overwhelmed her, but she resisted.

They had planned to go on a date tonight. She *had* to treat him as she would any other patient. If a nurse was attending the patient, as the chaplain, she would not enter the room.

If he were her boyfriend, she would go in though.

But if he were her boyfriend, she would have to wait to get permission to even enter the unit.

Grace sighed. She stepped away from the threshold and walked down the hall. Hitting the green button which opened the locked doors, she exited the Intensive Care Unit and offered up another prayer for Ches.

Beep. Beep. Beep.

Opening bleary eyes, Grace groped for the lamp next to her bed. She hit the switch and picked up her pager. The small screen declared a trauma patient would arrive at Regional Hospital in seven minutes as a result of an ATV.

All Terrain Vehicle.

It wasn't uncommon for people to ride ATVs when the weather was good.

Even at half past three in the morning.

As protocol required, Grace called the hospital to determine whether the page was necessary for her to come in. Chuck, the supervising nurse advised her.

"You better come in, Grace. This one's bad," he said.

"I'll be there in ten minutes," Grace said, throwing the covers off.

Grace met the family in the emergency room lobby and accompanied them to a smaller waiting room, offering them comfort and giving updates until they could go back into the department and see the patient, a seventeen year old male who had been driving his four wheeler too fast through the woods, and had lost control when he'd hit a hole.

At just shy of five in the morning, Grace walked down the Intensive Care Unit Hallway after accompanying the mother of the trauma patient to his room. Grace paused outside of room 410, though she wasn't sure why.

Fatigue had set in about an hour ago, so why was a little fuzzy.

Maria, the ICU nurse called to her. "Hey, Grace, you okay?"

Grace searched for something to say. She looked into the darkened room, the sliding glass door pulled mostly closed then walked over to the counter of the nurse's station.

"The patient in 410."

"Yes?"

Grace rested her arms on the counter top. "Is he yours?"

"Yes."

"I had a date with him tonight."

Maria smiled. "Did he stand you up, or is the date the reason he had a heart attack?"

Grace shook her head. "It was his birthday. I bought him work gloves, but when I got to his house, he wasn't there."

"Ah," she said in understanding. Maria's kind expression brought tears to Grace's eyes.

Grace tried to swallow past the lump in her throat and nodded. Maria stood. Without speaking, she walked around the desk and enfolded Grace in her arms.

Sweet Maria.

"Go in there and see him," Maria said against her hair.

Grace pulled away and swiped at her eyes. "It's not appropriate. I'm the chaplain. I'm on call."

"Which means if the hospital needs you, we will page you." Maria held out her hand. "Give me your badge."

"Why?"

"So you can be a friend to him. Go on."

"I shouldn't."

"You should. A patient is allowed one friend or family in the room at night. Mr. Larson has no one here."

Invisible tendrils of longing caused her to look toward the room.

"Go on, Grace. It's all right. He could definitely use a friend at his bedside. This is a terrible way to spend a birthday." Maria reached forward and unclasped Grace's badge from her blouse and clipped it on her scrub shirt. "If you need it back, call me."

Grace walked with trepidation to the room. Sliding open the door, she looked at the figure in the bed, lit by the numbers and lines on the monitor above him. His features were relaxed in sleep. She gripped the bedrail and closed her eyes.

"God," she whispered. "Please. Please help Ches. Comfort and protect Sunni and Haley. Surround all of them with your love."

Something touched her shoulders, and when Grace looked behind her, she saw Maria placing a folded blanket on her. She nodded toward the recliner in the corner. "Take a seat."

The recliner looked inviting.

"You'll be more comfortable praying there."

Maria's kindness warmed Grace. She moved to the chair and sat down. Maria opened a cabinet door and retrieved a pillow, handing it to Grace.

"Thank you." Grace slipped out of her shoes and tucked her feet under her. She set the pillow beside her and leaned against it.

She must have fallen asleep because when her pager vibrated against her hip, she awoke with a start. Grace placed her feet into her shoes and laying the blanket aside walked sedately out the door reading the small screen as she did so.

Uh-oh. Cardiac arrest in the E.R. now.

Chapter Five

Ches sat on the chair in the hospital room fighting the morose cloud surrounding him. He hated this place. Hated it.

Though the chair reclined, it was, of course, too short for his too-tall frame, so his feet hung over the foot rest.

He'd never been one to sit around and do nothing. But nothing was all he could do because they had taken his clothes and shredded them in the emergency room. All he had was a gown and too small hospital-issued socks to wear. It was humiliating. He'd never worn a gown in his life. Well, he hadn't been a patient in a hospital his entire life either, except for when he was born, and he certainly didn't remember that.

How long did he have to be here anyway? He'd lain on his back all night with no pillow scared to death if he moved he'd bleed out or the stents they'd put in would somehow become dislodged. He was used to propping on three pillows and sleeping on his side, never on his back. It had been the most uncomfortable night of his life. That was until Grace had come in. He must have dozed off, and in his dream Grace was beside him whispering. Then he was awake and realized she was praying.

Praying for him.

He hadn't spoken, wouldn't have been able to even if he had tried, he'd been so overcome with a deep gaping hopelessness for his life and a tenderness toward the woman for attempting to appeal to God on his behalf.

He'd never known anyone to pray for him.

It was humbling, and unnerving too.

But mostly it just made him sad because she was obviously kind—so good with Little Bit the night they'd met. If he was honest, he'd appreciated her beauty too. Her eyes that reminded him of the sky on a June day and her hair the color of wheat. He'd had a chance to get to know her better, but instead he'd ended up here as one of the patients she visited.

Jim, the nurse came in. Ches only knew his name because he'd came in with the breakfast tray and introduced himself. "How you doing?" Without waiting for an answer, he went past the chair and did something to the machine connected to the IV bag. The beeping Ches hadn't even noticed ceased.

"Chesapeake is an interesting name," he said, coming to stand next to Ches.

"I go by Ches."

"Are you named for the city?" The blood pressure cuff began to inflate.

"Yep." Ches didn't feel like sharing the story with the guy.

"Is the Grace on the wall the hospital chaplain?"

Ches' attention went to the dry erase board with Grace's, name, cell and extension numbers. The night nurse had written the information there shortly after Grace had left this morning though whether it was Grace's idea or the nurse's, Ches didn't know.

"Yep."

"How long y'all been going out?" The machine whined, and the band tightened uncomfortably around his bicep.

"Not long." Not like it was any of Jim's business.

"She working today?"

Ches shrugged, tired of the questions though he wouldn't mind knowing the answer to that one. It had been before daybreak that she'd been in his room, but he didn't know whether she was performing her pastoral duties or if their connection from the weekend before had compelled her to visit.

He wished he knew.

But did it really matter now? She wouldn't want to be saddled with a man with a weak heart.

As if his thoughts and Jim's comments summoned her, Grace walked in the room. Wearing a dark green knit top, blue jeans, and tennis shoes, with her hair in a ponytail, she looked like a co-ed. She smiled at him, and Ches had to stop his hand from going up to his chest to feel his thumping heart.

Unfortunately, the monitor picked up the accelerated heart rate. Ches hoped no one else noticed it, or at least the reason for it.

"Hi, Grace. I was just asking Ches about you."

"Oh?"

Uneasiness filled Ches. He stared at his long legs sticking out of the gown, his knees and lower legs bare ending in the ridiculous bottom-ridged socks on his gargantuan feet. He felt ridiculous and exposed.

Hey, everyone, come in and see the half-dressed heart patient.

Ches glanced at the neat folds of sheet and blanket on his bed, wishing he were close enough to grab them and cover up.

He didn't want Grace seeing his legs or wearing a gown. Her blue-jeaned frame moved across his line of vision as she stood next to the bed.

What was she doing?

Turning around, she held the blanket in her hands. Setting it on the arm of his chair, she moved away again. Shock wrestled with gratitude in Ches' craw as he unfolded the blanket and settled it over his legs and lap.

How had she known? How could she have possibly known?

He turned to watch her.

She stood on the other side of patient bed, her gaze roving around the room taking in every detail and stopping at the board where her name and number were recorded. Surprise flitted across her face before disappearing, giving Ches his answer about whether or not she had written it on there. "What did you want to know?" she asked Jim.

"Whether you were working today. I guess I have my answer as I've never seen you in jeans before."

Annoyance prickled at Ches as he thought Jim was flirting with his gal. Well, she wasn't exactly his gal, but Jim didn't know that.

She arched an eyebrow at the nurse. "Not all of us get to come to work in scrubs." Her attention turned to Ches, and her expression warmed, and something in Ches' chest relaxed. "How do you feel?" she asked.

"Ready to go home."

She put her hand on her hip. "They'll probably want to move you to a regular room first."

"I should be able to leave today."

Jim snorted, but Ches ignored him.

"I haven't seen the doctor yet, but that's what I'm going to tell him when he gets here."

"Her. Dr. Sondra Akeem."

Ches didn't remember a woman doctor. There had been a slew of people last night, and some of it was fuzzy.

"She and Dr. Ipstein were down the hall just now. You think they will come in here, Jim?"

"Yes," he answered.

She was so tall. Wicked tall, Little Bit had said. The thought made him smile. Out on the dance floor when they'd been holding Little Bit, Ches had decided Grace was the tallest woman he'd ever met. He liked that. He liked her.

"Great. Would it be okay if Ches and I talk alone before they come in?"

"Sure. Just behave. His heart rate shot up when you walked in. I don't want to have to call a code blue because you guys didn't have a chaperone."

Grace frowned at him.

"All right. All right. Point taken. You don't have to give me the death stare." Jim smirked at her before going to the door.

Grace crossed her arms over her chest and followed him out of the room. Shutting the sliding door, she paused outside of the room only her back visible, but it was ramrod straight. Through the small window next to the door, Ches caught a glimpse of Jim facing her. Interesting, the chaplain was having what Ches' daddy had called a coming-to-Jesus meeting with the nurse.

Grace entered the room a moment later with a pleasant smile on her face though Ches knew she had just put Jim through the ringer.

"What do you want me to do?" she asked.

He shook his head.

"Nothing?"

"I can't ask you to do anything, sugar," he said.

"You can ask me, but you're not comfortable asking me." She nodded. "All right. Let's try again. What do you need other than to be able to go home?"

Ches sighed. He didn't want to be obligated to this woman. He didn't want to ask her to do anything.

"I wish I had some pants. I don't like being in here with next to nothing on."

"It makes you feel vulnerable."

Ches pinched his lips. He didn't want to admit it to her, but yes.

"I could go to your house and pick up some of your clothes."

Ches imagined her going through his drawers, picking out underwear. He shook his head. "Nope."

"Call Sunni and ask her to bring your clothes?"

"I don't have my cell phone, and there's no phone in here."

"That's easy enough." She reached into her pocket and pulled out her phone. She offered it to him.

"Thanks." He dialed Sunni's number, but she didn't pick up. "Is it all right if I text her? She usually responds better with a text."

"Sure."

Ches kept it short and not too heavy on the details knowing Grace would be able to read the text later if she so wished. He told Sunni to bring him his phone, charger, and a change of clothes. He hit send and held the phone out to Grace. "I owe you an apology," he said.

"For what?"

"For missing our date."

Her mouth turned up in a smile, but it didn't reach her

eyes. "You were busy."

"How did you know I was here?"

"The chaplain on duty had to leave. He called to see if I would work for him. By that time, I realized we weren't going out, so I came to the hospital."

"You went to the house."

"Yes." She picked up a gift bag from the counter he hadn't noticed before. "This is for you, by the way." Dangling the handle on her extended fingers, she held it in front of him.

Surprised, he watched her face, those lovely blue eyes, almost gray now, studied him. He took the bag and glanced down into it. Two wrapped presents lay inside.

"The smaller one is for Haley."

Moved, Ches didn't speak. Yesterday was his birthday, and Grace had remembered. All kinds of feelings bubbled in his mind: frustration, gratitude, longing, despair.

"I'm not celebrating my birthday."

"Oh, go ahead and open it," she chided. "It was your birthday whether you celebrated it or not."

"I didn't want to be reminded. Especially now." Depression weighed on him. Not even 40 years old, and he'd had a heart attack. What would happen to Little Bit if something happened to him? The anxiety of it tore at him.

"Well, hurry up and open the present then, and I'll throw away the wrapping paper to destroy the evidence."

Setting the bag aside, Ches opened the gift, seeing a pair of work gloves in the flat box. He'd needed a pair, though how Grace could have possibly known that fact amazed him. He opened his mouth to ask her, but decided not to.

A knock sounded on the door, and a man and a woman in white lab coats entered. "Chesapeake Larson?" the woman said.

He nodded.

She extended her hand. "I'm Dr. Akeem. I am the one who placed your stents last night. This is my colleague Dr. Ipstein."

Jim followed them in and leaned on the counter. The doctor glanced at Grace.

"Hello. You are?"

"I'm Grace , I'm….umm."

Yeah, he felt the same way. "She's with me." That's all he could say. That's all he knew to say. He looked at Grace, the person with him. Date, friend, girlfriend, chaplain, companion, damsel on the side of the road, pray-er at his bedside, long-legged gentle woman with lovely sky blue eyes. He could use her calm strength, but he didn't know what was going to be said by the doctors. His pride had taken enough knocks since yesterday when the paramedics had shown up. He didn't want Grace to witness any more of his humiliation. "Grace? Would you come back and see me again?"

She nodded. She turned to go, walking to the door. Ches wondered if she really would come back.

"Grace?"

She stopped and looked over her shoulder, her hand already on the handle of the sliding door.

"This evening?"

"All right." She gazed at him a few seconds, and he wished he knew what she was thinking. Had his request made him an obligation to her? He hoped not.

Her hand moved the door open, and she was gone.

"How are you feeling today?" Dr. Akeem said.

Reluctantly he tore his eyes from the door. "Great. When can I get out of here?"

"Oh. Not for a few days yet. We want to monitor you before you are discharged."

"Why?"

"To be sure you respond well to the medication."

"What medication?"

"For your cholesterol and blood pressure. And a blood thinner. What medicines are you on presently?"

"I don't take any medicine."

Dr. Akeem looked at him over her glasses. "I mean what medicines were you taking before you were admitted to the hospital?"

Ches shook his head. "I wasn't."

"Not anything?"

"Nope."

"Surely, you take analgesics every once in a while. Nsaids?"

Ches looked at her. Why was it so hard to believe he didn't take medicine?

"Aspirin then?"

Another negative movement from him.

"What do you take when you have a headache or strain your back?" she said in disbelief.

Ches clamped down the irritation threatening to gurgle into his throat. Patiently, he spoke. "I drink coffee for a headache, and I soak in the tub for a backache. I don't take medicine. I never have."

"You'll have to take medicine now," Dr. Akeem proclaimed. "Your blood pressure is high and so is your cholesterol."

Ches didn't reply. They can tell him whatever they wanted. It didn't mean he had to do it. "So, when can I leave?"

****

Grace sent another text to Sunni identifying herself and saying she was going to be close by and would stop in to pick up the things Ches had said he needed. She waited a half hour then called.

"What?" Sunni snapped as a greeting.

"Hi, this is Grace. I sent you a text."

"Yes. I saw it."

"I will be by the house in 30 minutes to pick up your dad's things." Usually Grace wouldn't insist on stopping by someone's house, but Sunni was either unaware of how important it was to Ches to have his things, or else she didn't care. "Did you find his phone?"

"Yeah."

"See you in a little while."

"Great," she said sarcastically.

Grace made it there in twenty-seven minutes. As she pulled in front of the house, Haley ran from the front porch, her face shining with glee.

"Miss Grace! Miss Grace!"

Grace exited the car, and Haley grabbed her around her legs hugging her tightly. Her blonde hair was matted in two places testifying that it hadn't been brushed recently. Grace bent down and picked her up and held her close to her.

"How are you?"

"We are awful. All we eat is sandwiches."

Grace walked toward the front porch. "Hopefully, it won't be too long before Pop gets home."

"I sure miss him."

The door opened, and Sunni stood there in a thin T-shirt and jeans which were more fray than denim.

Grace smiled in greeting. "Hi."

She looked Grace up and down. "Did Dad send you to check on us?"

"No. He doesn't know I'm here. But they cut his clothes in the ER, and he doesn't have anything to wear. I had some extra time, and don't mind taking him what he needs unless you're going?"

Sunni pinched her lips together. "What am I supposed to do with Haley if I go to the hospital?"

"If you want to see your dad, Haley can stay with me," Grace offered. She stepped forward and took another step. Sunni had no choice but to move out of the way. She opened the door wider, reluctantly allowing Grace in the house.

Grace glanced about the room. It looked as if Haley's toy box had exploded. Grace set Haley down and wondered how offended Haley would be if Grace started cleaning up.

"Tomorrow I'll be going to Miss Aretha's. You can go see Pop then, Sissy."

"I'll be in school then. I won't have time. He expects me to have perfect grades. As if anyone can thrive when he keels over and ends up in Intensive Care and wants me to take care of every single thing."

"Let me help, Sunni."

She huffed, and her eyes glittered, but whether it was from anger or tears, Grace couldn't tell. "You can't fix what's wrong here."

"Probably not, but I can take what Ches needs to him, so you don't have to. You'll let me do that, won't you?" Grace watched the young woman and waited for her answer, her permission.

"I wish I could go see Pop. Don't you think you could sneak me in, Miss Grace?" Her gaze—so much like Pop's—appealed to Grace, making her want to do exactly as the child asked.

"I'm sorry, honey."

"Maybe you can take a picture of me so he won't be so lonesome."

"That sounds like a good idea."

"Great!" Haley danced around the room enthusiastically. "Here. One with me and Jojo." She stopped, closed her eyes, and inhaled. Opening her mouth wide, she yelled, "Jojo!" Jojo obeyed the summons and appeared in the room.

Grace retrieved her cellular phone from her purse and took several pictures of Haley with and without Jojo. "What about you, Sunni? Want me to take a picture of you for your dad?"

She had sat down in the corner of the couch and had her eyes trained on her own phone. "He doesn't want a picture of me."

"Are you sure?"

"Yep."

Grace aimed her cell phone at her and took a couple anyway. Sunni was so engrossed on her phone that she didn't notice. Grace decided seeing his daughter looking at the screen of her phone would be an image familiar to Ches, so it should comfort him.

After taking a quick inventory of the duffel bag Haley

had packed for Ches, Grace headed out of Wren's Holler to Regional Hospital.

When she arrived in the Intensive Care Unit, she stopped at the nurse's station. It was nearly eight in the evening which meant the shift change had occurred. Grace was somewhat relieved. Jim liked to tease her, and she wasn't in the mood to deal with him where Ches was concerned. Debbie sat behind the desk, and Grace noted on the board that she was assigned to Ches. Grace liked all of the nurses in ICU, though some she knew better than others.

But, Grace really liked Debbie. She was one of the best night nurses on the unit.

"I'm not here as a chaplain," Grace said.

"Oh?"

"Ches is a friend."

She wrinkled her forehead. "Ches?"

"Chesapeake Larson. Room 410."

"Oh. I haven't had him before. I just got report from Jim. He's ornery."

"This is news? I thought everyone knew that about Jim."

Debbie shook her head. "I'm talking about your friend. He's refusing meds."

"What?"

"He won't take anything. He's even complaining about the IV."

"What does Dr. Akeem say?"

"We haven't called her yet."

"Why not?"

"She'll be here in the morning. His BP isn't dangerously high. Otherwise, Jim would have, and so would I."

"Do you know why he won't take the medicine?"

Debbie shrugged. "Do you?"

Grace shook her head.

"Want to find out?"

"I can ask."

"Maybe convince him he needs to."

Grace picked up the duffel which lay resting on the floor. Resolutely, she turned to the room.

Ready for battle, chaplain? A voice within her mind asked.

I'm not his chaplain. I'm his friend, she answered.

Ready for battle, friend?

Grace closed her eyes, and words from a Psalm filled her mind.

Blessed be the Lord, my rock, who trains my hands for war, and my fingers for battle.

She opened her eyes and slid the door wide enough to walk through. The curtain was pulled, and she knocked on the plastic sanitizer dispenser mounted on the wall. "Ches? It's Grace. May I come in?"

"Sure."

Grace walked around the curtain and saw Ches standing behind his bed and the wall of glass at the back of the room. He had his back to her, and she noted he had a hospital gown on backwards, using it as a robe. A metal IV pole stood next to him, and cords trailed on the floor from him to the monitors, displaying his heart and respiratory rate, and oxygen level. In the low light of the room, the window acted as a mirror, and Grace saw her reflection set his bag on the bed and approach his reflection. Standing a few feet behind him, she looked through the plate glass window at the hues of sunset over the city.

"I've often thought they should turn the patient beds around to face the window instead of the door. It's such a lovely view that would benefit the patient, I think."

"Why don't they?"

"If the bed faces away from the door, the staff can't see the patient as well, and they cannot attend to the patient as well either, especially in an emergency situation."

They stood in silence for a few moments. Grace wondered if he was going to speak at all. Did he want her here? Words and phrases flitted around in her head, but she resisted vocalizing any of them.

Silence was often an important moment in a room. It

gave witness to one's pain, one's heartache. Grace had learned in her work as a chaplain that if she attended to the silence, it allowed the patient time and opportunity to recognize what they were feeling so that they could then express it.

"I feel like a prisoner."

Grace waited for more.

Ches turned to her. "The only other time I've ever been a patient in a hospital was when I entered this world 39 years ago."

"It's not a role you're used to."

"No, and it's not one I like."

"It won't be for long."

"It's already too long."

"I brought you some clothes. Do you think you'd feel more comfortable in something you own?"

He let out a pent up breath, and his mouth opened in a smile creasing his whisker roughened cheeks. "Bless you, Grace. Yes."

They walked toward the bed, and Grace went further, switching on the overhead light. Ches opened the bag, and removed the T-shirt and sweat pants Sunni had packed.

"You're not going to walk out of here, are you?"

"Don't tempt me."

Grace laughed. "I'll step out a few minutes. Press the nurse button if you need Debbie." She left and went out to the nurse's station. Debbie went in a few minutes later, then returned giving Grace the go ahead. When Grace entered, Ches sat on the bed dressed in the sweat pants and T-shirt. At a glance, Grace could see his relaxed continence.

The bag sat next to him, and his cell phone was plugged up and on the mobile bed tray next to him.

"Better?"

"Yep."

Grace sat on the chair near the bed. "Good."

He moved his fingers across the screen on his phone. "Did you see Sunni?"

"Yes."

"I just texted her. I'd really like to talk to Little Bit." He sighed. "I doubt Sunni will respond to me, and Little Bit doesn't have a phone."

"Can you call the house phone?"

Ches' eyebrows went up. "Good idea." In a moment he held the cell phone to his ear. His lips turned up. "Hey Young 'um. This is your pop."

Grace heard a squeal from the phone and animated chatter. "I miss you. Miss you bunches." He listened, responded to her questions, some of which included Grace. From his side of the conversation, Grace knew Haley was telling him about her visit, and the injustice of having to eat sandwiches and Spaghettios for lunch and supper. Ches assured her he'd be home as soon as he could, and finished the conversation with, "I know, and I'm sorry. We'll catch up on all our good night reading when I get home. I promise. I promise. I love you, Little Bit. Good night." He ended the call with a sigh. "I've never been away from her for this long before. Not since she came to live with us."

"It's hard." Grace acknowledged the truth she knew Ches was feeling.

He scrubbed his face with his hands.

"She's counting on you to be around for a long time, you know." Grace pulled up the pictures of Haley she had taken earlier in the day. She leaned forward and offered the phone to him. He took the phone and looked at the picture.

"There's more there. Just move your finger to the right and you can see the next one."

He did so, moving through several of them. He gave a brief chuckle of amusement. "I see you captured Sunni in her favorite pose."

"They need you, Ches."

"I know."

"They need you."

Ches turned to her, his eyebrow arched. Waiting for her to make her point.

"If you don't take your medicine, you are not going to

be here to take care of them."

"Any amount of medicine is not going to keep me here if it's my time to go."

"Agreed, but high blood pressure can cause a stroke. If you're lucky, it will kill you quickly. If you're not, you'll lose the ability to speak or move, depending on which part of the brain the stroke happens. You will not be able to take care of Sunni and Haley if you are disabled. High cholesterol can cause another heart attack. It damages your heart and will weaken you so that you can't run, can't even walk very far. How are you going to manage your farm if you can't walk more than twenty feet?"

He leaned back against the raised head of the bed, closing his eyes.

"I have seen what high blood pressure and high cholesterol can do to a person."

Without looking at her, he raised his hand with her phone in a gesture for her to take it. "Thank you, Chaplain. I will take your words under advisement."

Grace didn't take her phone. "No." He was not going to get off this easy. "I am not your chaplain. I am a chaplain here, yes, but I'm here in this room tonight because I care about you."

He lowered his hand and set the phone next to his on the table. "You're a chaplain so you care about everybody. That's your job."

"It's not my job tonight. Carol is the chaplain at Regional right now. I don't work again until Monday."

"Thanks for bringing my clothes, Grace."

It was a dismissal. Ches still hadn't opened his eyes. Desperation gripped her. Why was he being so stubborn? Didn't he know he could die?

"I do care about you," she said. "I do."

"You feel sorry for me."

"I'm feeling a lot of things right now. Pity isn't one of them." He must have heard the anger in her tone, because he finally opened his eyes. He leaned forward, his face turned toward her. "If it doesn't sway you that I care about you, I can handle that. But I also care about Haley, and Sunni, too, although she's not an easy person to like. I imagine a lot of her attitude is that she's scared to death you're going to die and leave her. Your stubborn refusal to take medicine that could keep you healthy and alive is going to cost Sunni her dad and Little Bit her pop. Please take the medicine, Ches."

"You're hitting below the belt."

"I'm not your opponent. The heart disease is. Fight it."

"My own genes are fighting against me. I won't win this."

"Why do you say that?"

"My dad dropped dead at 39. So did my granddad. I'm not going to make it to 40, Sugar. No male in our family ever has."

Tears smarted at the back of her eyes at the dejection in his expression.

"You are going to break the pattern."

"I wish I believed you."

Chapter Six

That night Grace lay in the bed thinking of Ches. He thought he was dying, that there was no hope he would live to see his 40s. Grace had thought reminding him of the love of his children would be enough incentive to take care of himself, but it hadn't been. What else could she do?

She sighed and turned on her side, seeing the nighttime sky through her bedroom window.

Is there anything I can do, Lord, to make him see?

No answer came, but a calm filled her. She watched the nighttime clouds move slowly across the dark canvas. She did care about Ches, but only he could decide to live, to fight what genetics had handed him with the knowledge and skill God had revealed through science and medicine.

As a chaplain, Grace could bring comfort and support and encourage him to follow the treatment plan.

As a woman who had a date with him three days ago, perhaps she could do more. Visit him when she wasn't working. Help him with Haley and Sunni. And maybe something else, but what, she wasn't sure yet.

The next day, she arrived at work and began her visits in the emergency department as was her routine. Early in the afternoon when a code blue came over the P.A. system, Grace paused. As the chaplain, she was a first responder though not to attend the patient, but any family who might be present.

Code Blue, Room 410.

Every nerve ending exploded in her body, and Grace ran to the elevator.

It took an eternity, or seemed to, for the elevator to arrive. A tech approached pushing a portable ECG machine, also one of the first responders for a code.

Oh, please. Oh, please, God, don't let him die.

The elevator doors opened, and they entered. In less than a minute, they were on the fourth floor. Grace hurried to the doors of ICU and slid her id badge through the security device to gain access, but it didn't open. She ran it through again and again. The light still showed red.

"Here let me," the ECC tech said. She ran her card, the light changed to green, and the door opened.

Grace shot through the door, turned the corner, and saw the crowd of staff spilling out of the room and gathered in the hallway. Fear and determination accompanied her as she approached the room. Debbie, one of the nurses, saw her.

"No family," she said.

Grace craned her head to see in the room. Though the door was open all the way, the curtain obstructed most of the bed, but not the legs of the nurse doing CPR. A machine signaled the alarm for a flatline.

Someone grabbed her upper arm and she turned. It was Jim, all mirth gone from his face. "It's not him," he said. "They moved him to stepdown this morning about three. This guy came in through the ED last night in critical condition. It's not your boyfriend, so calm down."

Grace shook her head trying to understand the nurse's words.

"I don't remember his room number. You'll have to look it up."

"It's not Ches?"

"No."

On shaky legs, Grace went to the nurse's station and sat down. She logged into the computer and searched for Ches.

467.

She stared at the name and number.

It's not him. It's not him.

Jim appeared at the counter in front of her. "There's nothing for you to do here. Go see him."

Anger and gratitude prickled at her. "This is really none of your business, you know."

"Oh, come on. You know I'm a sucker for good love story. Go on. Go on now."

Grace arose. She walked around the counter to stand

in front of Jim. "Thanks for letting me know." Without waiting for his reply, she exited the unit to find Ches.

His door was shut, and Grace knocked on it firmly then entered. Ches sat on the bed dressed in the sweats and T she'd seen him in the day before, one leg crooked and the other stretched out in front of him. His face registered surprise.

"I want my date," she declared. "I want my date with you, so, yes, you are going to take your medicine. Today. As soon as they can bring it in this room. Even if I have to shove it down your throat. Do you understand?"

His gaze shifted from her for a moment then back. "Yeah, Sugar. I understand."

"And you are going to take your medicine, right?"

He nodded, a small smile upturning his lips.

"Good." At a loss for how easily he had capitulated, Grace crossed her arms over her chest. "I'll go get the nurse." She turned and nearly collided into a woman in scrubs. Her badge identified her as Julie, one of the cardiac stepdown nurses. "Oh."

Julie glanced at Grace's badge. "Pastoral care, huh? What are you doing, putting the fear of God into him?"

"The fear of Grace," Ches said. "Ain't that right, sugar?"

Heat radiated over Grace's face. She gestured with her thumb over her shoulder. "I know him."

"Are you his ride? The doctor said he could go home, but I don't have the discharge papers yet."

"He needs his medicine."

Julie looked at Ches. "What medicine? I don't have any new orders for him."

"For his...." Grace searched for the right words, knowing she was overstepping boundaries. "His blood pressure and...such."

"He's already had it. I gave it to him myself early this morning."

"You did?"

"That's right, and he took it like an obedient and

compliant patient. No shoving down the throat required, right, Mr. Larson?"

"Yep."

The urge to run out of the room to escape the mortification Grace felt blanketed her. But she plowed on. "My shift at the hospital ends at four." She pinned Julie with a firm stare. "Call the doctor now and tell her to stop by the unit and sign the discharge order. Immediately. Maybe if you tell her it's urgent, she might do it within the next three hours." Then to Ches. "I will be back shortly after four to take you home."

It was a strange side of Grace, this aggressive creature who had marched into that room and demanded her way.

She didn't offer. She didn't ask.

She just told Ches that's how it was going to be, even threatened him, and he hadn't argued.

It was a side of herself she hadn't met before. Jokingly, Ches had said she had put the fear of Grace into him, and well, he wasn't far from the truth, because she had been afraid.

Afraid he'd give up on living, and she wouldn't have the chance to get to know him, maybe even be a part of his life. And she wanted to be. Or at least the chance to explore what could be. Because she could see herself fitting in with their lives. She could see it pretty clearly.

In the car on the way to Wren's Holler, Grace wondered what had happened to her alter ego. Aggressive Grace would have known what to say in the confines of the car on the half hour trek. Even Chaplain Grace should know topics of conversation to fill awkward silences, but what to say to a man you'd ordered to take his medicine so he'd be well enough to take you out on a date whether he wanted to or not?

Ches didn't speak either.

She glanced over at him. His head was leaned back on the seat, and his eyes were closed. But he wasn't asleep because his fingers tapped his thigh to the tune of the radio.

When she passed the place where she'd driven off the

road to avoid the deer, Ches finally spoke.

"Bring back memories?"

"Yes."

"Me too."

"What do you remember?" Grace asked.

She glanced at him, and found he was watching her. "I suppose I ought to make a confession."

"Oh?"

"Yep. I have chain I carry in my toolbox on my truck. I could have gotten you out of the ditch that day, but I didn't even offer, didn't even try other than a half-hearted attempt to get your car back on the road. And the whole time I knew that chain was there. Now, wasn't that awful of me?"

Why hadn't he pulled the car out with the chain and his truck?

"I'm sure you had a good reason for not getting the car out of the ditch."

He smiled. Grace turned her attention back to the road before she ended up in the ditch again.

"I sure did."

He wasn't going to say why. Not without her asking him outright apparently.

"Well, what was it?"

She maneuvered the car into his driveway. He waited until she put the gear in park and turned to him.

"I thought it would be more fun to go to the wedding. If I'd pulled your car out, Little Bit and I wouldn't have had an excuse to accompany you, now would we?" He clicked his safety belt, opened the door, and exited the vehicle.

Grace followed his example, and over the roof of the car, she watched him stretch like a cat just awake from a nap.

A dog barked insistently, then Jojo appeared from the corner of the house and bounded to Ches who held up his hands defensively. "Hey Jojo, now don't knock me down, boy. Sit. Sit."

The dog sat obediently, his adoring eyes gazing at

Ches, and his wagging tail creating a cloud of dust. Ches bent down and petted his massive head, then scratched his ears. "It's good to be home." He turned to Grace. "Want to come in? I can't vouch for the state of the house. Probably looks like a tornado tore through it." He began walking to the front porch with Jojo at his side. Grace followed.

Inside the house, his prediction wasn't far off. Toys and clothes strewn on the furniture and floor.

"Pop!" Haley ran to Ches and launched herself in his arms. He picked her up, hugging her tightly.

"Oh, I missed you," he said against her hair. Leaning back a bit, he kissed her cheek and grinned at her. "Missed you something fierce."

"I missed you too. What are we having for supper?"

"Oh, I'll have to see what we have. Where's Sissy?"

"In her room, of course."

Ches kissed her cheek one more time and set her on the floor. "You get your toys picked up and put away, and I'll get us something to eat."

"Aww, man. How come I gots to clean up now?"

"Because you didn't do it before."

Ches walked toward the stairs, and Haley caught sight of Grace. "Miss Grace! How'd you get here?"

"I brought Pop home."

Haley wrapped her arms around Grace's legs and squeezed. "I didn't think this day would ever come," she said against Grace's knee. Looking up, she gave Grace a pouty face. "It's been awful without Pop, and now he's making me clean up. Want to help me?"

Grace snickered. "I could probably do that."

Haley released her and dropped her shoulders in relief. "Oh, good, cause this place is a wreck, and I'm only five, you know."

Grace put her hands on her hips and surveyed the room. "Do all of these toys belong in here?"

Haley mimicked her pose. "No. Some go in my room."

"You pick up the toys that go in the box over there, and I'll work on the clothes and shoes. Then we'll take what's leftover and take them to your bedroom. All right?"

"Great."

Grace folded the clothes strewn on the couch and gathered socks attempting to match them. She reminded Haley to stay on task when the little girl would stop and play with the toys she was supposed to be putting away.

Haley knelt beside a large basket which served as storage for her things. "Miss Grace?"

"Yes?"

"If we do a good job, will you play in the ball pit with me?"

"You have a ball pit?"

"Yeah. On the back porch."

"Sure."

"Pop made it for me because I kept bugging him to take me to Slouchy Joe's so I could play in theirs. But someone had an accident in it, and he said it was safer if I just played in one at home."

Grace laid socks out across the couch cushions. How could there be eighteen socks without mates?

"Did someone get hurt?" she asked absently.

"No, someone peed. Pop said some kids are too busy playing to realize they need to go potty. But I don't have that problem."

Grace grinned. "That's good."

"Mainly, it's cause Pop reminds me to go. He's good that way. Are you going to eat supper with us?"

"Oh. Well. I hadn't really thought about it."

Footsteps on the stairs brought Grace's attention to where Ches entered the room from the second story. He'd changed clothes, and his damp hair and freshly shaven face attested he'd freshened up before tackling dinner. In blue jeans, a black T-shirt, and bared feet, Ches' appearance caused Grace to lose her breath. She turned away from him and stared hard at the socks.

He paused as he walked by. "Did she con you into helping her?"

"What do you think?"

"I didn't con nobody. I asked nicely," Haley defended.

"Hmm-mmm." Ches tone demonstrated his skepticism. He studied the socks, tutted, and scooped them up with one fell swoop, fisting them in his hand. "Sugar, are you staying for supper?"

Grace examined his face for a hint as to whether he was practicing good manners or if he wanted her to stay. There was something there. Tension, perhaps. She couldn't name it. A sweet tangy scent meandered in the air. Subtle, but nice. His soap, perhaps. She inhaled.

Stay! A voice within her urged. You can sniff him some more.

She tilted her face a bit to meet his eyes. Gosh, it was nice to have to look up to someone.

Haley grabbed her hand and pulled. "You have to play in the ball pit even if you don't stay for supper."

Whatever spell his proximity had woven popped like a soap bubble. "I probably should go. You have enough to do without worrying about feeding a guest."

He shrugged and walked toward the kitchen. "We'd love to have you. Though I imagine the same inclement weather which struck the rest of the house probably left a disaster in the kitchen as well." He stopped at the threshold. Shaking his head, he continued in the room.

Hmm. How bad was it?

Grace picked up Haley and followed Ches. Dishes filled the double sink, and pots containing food sat on the stained stove.

"Glad she fed you, at least," Ches growled. He opened the dish washer and picked up a bowl. Examining it, he opened a cabinet and set it on the bare shelf.

"Pizza, pizza, pizza," Haley chanted.

"That's an idea although…." Grace didn't finish. Pizza wasn't the healthiest choice, but she didn't want to overstep her bounds by voicing it.

Ches continued unloading the dishwasher, but he smiled. "Although I'm sure that won't be good for my cholesterol."

"Do you have any fixings for salad? It could offset the pizza."

"Yep. I had just gone grocery shopping when...."

An odd tone had entered his voice, but his back was to Grace.

"When?" she prompted.

"When I had the heart attack."

"I thought it was when you and Sissy was arguing, Pop."

He dropped his head for a second. Then his shoulders straightened and he turned to face them. If there was any anxiety or regret in him, he hid it well. "Pizza sounds like a great idea."

"Let's do it," Haley said.

"Do they deliver this far out?" Grace asked him.

"No, but I could go pick it up if you want to try out the ball pit with Little Bit."

He hadn't mentioned Sunni, though Haley had. He hadn't acknowledged the little girl's statement that he and Sunni had been arguing when he'd had the heart attack. It fit Sunni's feelings the day she'd met her at the hospital. She'd said it was her fault. And though Grace knew Ches' daughter didn't cause the attack, the way he processed tension and stress of their relationship could have been a contributing factor.

Ches picked up the telephone and ordered the pizza. While he spoke, Grace closed her eyes to pray.

Lord, help me know how to be a blessing to Ches and his family. Whatever is going on with Ches and Sunni, please help them to be reconciled to each other, mend their relationship.

She felt Haley's hand on her cheek. She shifted in Grace's arms. "What are you doing?"

Grace opened her eyes and found Haley's face close to hers.

"I was praying."

A look of disbelief came across her features. "I thought people only prayed at bedtime and on Thanksgiving."

Grace set her on the floor and took her hand. "Show me to the ball pit."

When Haley began to lead her through the house, Grace spoke. "Perhaps some people only pray at bedtime or on Thanksgiving, but I find I have to pray more often than that. Paul says we are to pray without ceasing."

"Who's Paul?"

"He was a man who wrote letters, and the letters are in the Bible."

They walked through the living room to a set of double French doors. Haley opened one, and they descended two stairs to a brick-floored screened-in high-ceilinged porch. In the corner was a mesh tent, its floor covered with colorful balls.

"Wow. This is neat."

"We take our shoes off," Haley said.

When they stood in stockinged feet, Haley took hold of the clasp and opened the massive zipper serving as the door. She stepped through the flap and motioned for Grace to enter. After unzipping the opening further, Grace entered and they sat amidst the balls.

Haley moved behind her and zipped the tent closed. "Which letters?"

"What?"

"What letters did Paul write in the Bible? Like A,B,C,D, or what?

Grace smiled. "No, letters to people. Does Pop or Sunni ever text someone on their cell phones?"

"Sunni does all the time."

"A letter is like a text, but longer. Paul told people things about Jesus to encourage them."

"Why didn't he just talk to them?"

"He was in prison or in another city, so he couldn't talk to them. He had to write the letters, and I'm so glad he did because now we can read them and be encouraged too. So, what do we do in this ball pit? Just sit here?"

"No, you can pretend you're a worm and crawl through them. That's fun. Or throw them around. Pop built me a big tic-tac-toe board. Want to play?"

"Sure."

Haley stood and waded over to one side where a foam square had the familiar tic-tac-toe lines across it. Each square was a net basket, closed at the bottom.

"You can either throw them in the basket or you can just put them in there. Usually when Pop and I play, we throw them cause he says it's good hand eye cord-nation. That means it helps you throw better."

"I see."

"So, you want to throw them or just put them in there?"

"Let's throw them. I'm all for good hand eye cord-nation."

"Okay. You have to get the same color ball to use every time you throw. I'll be purple."

"I'll be green. Who goes first?"

"You go first since you're the guest."

"Thanks."

They played until Haley decided she'd had enough and began throwing different color balls, confusing the game.

"Want to see something cool?" Grace asked.

"Yeah."

Grace picked up three balls and straightened, balancing on her knees. She juggled the balls.

"Oh, my gosh, Miss Grace!" Haley squealed.

When one of the balls fell, Grace smiled down at the little girl. "Pretty neat, huh?"

"Wicked neat. How did you learn to do that?"

"I took a class in fun."

"You think you could teach me?"

"It's easier to learn with bean bags. Why don't I bring you some next time I come over?"

"All right."

Grace reached down and felt the floor. "This is soft." She attempted to part the balls so she could see what she was kneeling on. But more rolled into the ravine she attempted to make. "What's under here?"

"Only one way to find out," Haley said, then disappeared.

Grace followed her example, lying back and wriggling down under the plastic spheres, then inching toward the little-girl giggles. When she found her, Haley had curled up hiding her eyes behind her hands. Grace pulled her cell phone out of her pocket and turned on the flashlight. "I see you."

Haley squealed again, her body exploding in movement, arms and legs flailing excitedly. Balls flew around with her gesticulations. Grace scooted away to avoid getting kicked.

"Where'd you go?" Haley asked, becoming still suddenly.

"I'm here."

"Don't leave me."

"I won't, sweetie."

Grace heard the hollow clicking of plastic as Haley moved nearer to her.

"We can put our heads on the edge and pretend we're in a bubble bath. Want to?"

"Sure."

Graced noted the bottom was made up of a multi-colored pad of interlocking pieces made of soft foam. Moving to settle against the low cushioned edge of the pit, they reclined side by side.

"Miss Grace?"

"Yes?"

"Is Pop going back to the hospital tonight?"

"No. They said he could come home and stay here."

"I don't want him to go back there. Ever."

"It was scary, wasn't it?"

Haley looked up at the ceiling, her chest heaved a sigh big enough to displace several balls. "Yes." They sat for a few moments in silence, then, "Do you know where Heaven is?"

"Why do you ask?"

"Sissy said Pop was going to die, like my mom did. If

Pop dies, he'll go to heaven, and I won't see him ever again."

Obviously, Ches' heart attack had brought up feelings of loss and fear for the little girl.

"If he dies, I want to die too. That way, I can be with him and my mama. So, I'm going to make sure I die as soon as I can."

Chapter Seven

Grace let the horror of Haley's words wash over her. "How are you going to die as soon as you can?"

"I'm going to have a heart attack like Pop. If you get Sissy to scream at you long enough, you fall down, and if 911 doesn't come get you, you die."

"Huh." Grace reached over, and finding Haley's hand, she held it. "Can I tell you something about Pop and Sunni?"

"Yeah."

"Your pop, he loves you. And Sunni loves you, too. And even though they get mad at each other, they love each other. Sunni screaming at him didn't really make him have the heart attack. She actually saved his life when she called 911. Your pop's heart just needed some extra help doing its work, and until he had the attack, no one knew it. But now we know, and he went to the doctor so the doctor could tell him what to do to make his heart work like it's supposed to. You don't have to worry now that he's going to die. He's going to be okay, and he'll see you grow up like Sunni is, and maybe one day you'll have a little girl just like you, and she can call him Pop, too. Won't that be neat?"

"Yeah."

"It's good you told me all of this. Any time you are scared about something, you can tell me or Pop because it helps to talk about it."

"What if you're not here?"

"I can give you my phone number, and you can call me."

"I have to ask to use the phone cause sometimes I press the wrong buttons, and people don't know me."

"Anyone who doesn't know you is really missing out, you know that?"

Haley laughed.

"Ladies?" Ches called. "The pizza is here if you're hungry."

Haley scrambled toward the zippered door of the tent and opening it, she jumped through it, and in a flash she was gone. Grace followed, and found three pizza boxes on the table, a stack of four plates beside four forks, and a large wooden bowl filled with salad next to several bottles of dressing.

When they were settled at the table, Haley announced, "We need to pray without sneezing."

Ches' brow furrowed briefly, then he nodded. "All right, Little Bit. Go for it."

Haley closed her eyes, so Grace bowed her head, closed her eyes, and waited.

"Dear Jesus, help us not to sneeze or to have snotty noses. Amen."

"Far be it from me to complain about your prayer—I'm for good health and all—but folks usually just thank the Lord for the food before they eat," Ches said.

"We don't."

Ches stared at Haley, and she stared back with the sincere honesty only a child can get away with. He shook his head with a sigh, admitting defeat. Turning to Grace, his gave her a self-deprecating smile, "Sugar, do you usually pray before meals?"

"Yes."

"Perhaps you could show Little Bit how it's done."

Grace once again bowed her head. "Gracious God, for what we are about to eat, let us be truly thankful. Amen."

Finishing the prayer, they began to eat. Grace noted the unused plate and fork on the table. She resisted the urge to ask if the young woman upstairs in her room knew Ches was home or that he had brought pizza for supper.

Sunni and Ches had a long history which Grace knew nothing about. She had no business coming into his home as a guest and suggesting he go upstairs and invite his own daughter down to eat.

Maybe he already had.

After supper, Haley patted her stomach. "I'm full. Pop, can we walk around the pond?"

Ches glanced at the clock on the wall. "It's getting late. You need to be in bed soon."

"Oh, please? Miss Grace hasn't seen the pond yet."

Ches pursed his lips in thought. He looked at the clock again, then that verdant gaze laid upon Grace. He arched an eyebrow in inquiry.

"Perhaps a short walk," Grace said.

"Yes!" Haley crowed.

"Get your shoes on. With socks. I just put a heap of socks in the clothesbasket in the pantry. Pull out two of them, and maybe by some miracle, you'll get a matched set."

"But don't hold your breath," Haley called over her shoulder as she shot out of her chair and through the kitchen.

Ches stood and began gathering the used dishes. "I won't hold my breath."

Grace closed the pizza boxes. She picked them up.

"Just leave them," he said.

"Are you sure?" She set the boxes back down on the table.

His gaze strayed to the doorway of the living room and up as if he were looking at the stairs. His gaze returned to her. He nodded. "I'll take care of it later." He walked to the dishwasher and sorted the plates, forks, and glasses into the appliance.

Ches and Grace walked side by side in the soft grass near the pond as Haley chased lightning bugs beginning their courtship ritual in the twilight of the evening. A rising and falling chorus of insects Ches had identified as cicadas accompanied Haley's squeals. Grace watched her closely, a little uneasy about how close she ran to the water's edge. Once when the little girl fell near the cat tails, Grace had intercepted her, moving in between her and the water.

"Sweetie, I wish you wouldn't get so close to the water. It makes me nervous," Grace said.

"I do this all the time," Haley said rolling across the ground with arms stretched above her head.

Grace knelt before her watching her. She sighed, not liking Haley's message. "You don't do this all the time without Pop here, do you?"

"Watch this! I can roll all the way across to the bench." And she did so.

Ches approached Grace, and holding his hand down to her, he helped her to her feet. "She's not allowed past the gate unless I'm with her."

His warm hand engulfed hers, the callused palm firm against her softer skin.

Grace entwined her fingers through his though the safety of Haley occupied her mind. "You don't worry about her not obeying you?"

He shook his head. "She knows she isn't allowed. I've never had a problem with her disobeying me."

"What about Sunni?"

Ches shook his head. "After her mother sent her back to me, something changed in Sunni. It's like I couldn't love her enough for what Vanessa did."

Grace wanted to ask what had happened the day Ches had had the heart attack, but she didn't. Ches had to trust her enough to tell her without her asking him.

"It must feel like to her that Vanessa had left both of you."

Ches watched Haley as she caught a bug and placed him in an empty mayonnaise jar he'd given her before they left the house. "She did leave both of us. Sunni cried herself to sleep every night. For months. She didn't want me to comfort her, hold her even. It was a hard time for both of us. Not that I missed my wife that much at that point. Having Vanessa decide to leave was a relief in a way. But I had no idea what our divorce would do to Sunni. If I had known...." He sighed.

"What would you have done?"

"I would have tried harder to convince her to stay, or at least when she left, I wouldn't have let her take Sunni."

They stood for a moment absorbing the truth of Ches' statement. Finally, he tugged on her hand and called out to

Haley. "Little Bit? Come on. It's time for bed."

Obediently, she ran toward Ches, her hair flying around her young face. "Pop, you think we can have a camp out?"

"Some time, but it'll take some planning. Come on now." He began the trek toward the house. Haley fell into step next to Grace, taking her hand.

Warmth spread through Grace as she walked between man and girl. This was significant. A connection formed between her and Ches, one that had begun the night they met, but strengthened at the hospital. Grace often prayed at the bedside of patients, asking for healing and protection. She considered that time a service of her job, a small anonymous print on each person's life, a privilege to ask for a divine blessing for health and wholeness, but most of the time she never met the patients again.

Not so with Chesapeake Larson.

Maybe because she'd known him first as a person, a Good Samaritan, the Pop to Haley.

And as a man with a husky honeyed voice who had taken her breath away in a buttoned down shirt, khakis, and cowboy boots.

She'd had a stake in praying for Ches. Her prayers had been on his behalf, but for hers as well, because she had already known him. And wanted to keep knowing him. Wanted to know him better, closer, deeper.

The potential of what could be appeared before her like the first stars visible in the evening sky.

She recognized the hope and kept walking forward. Felt the squeeze of Ches' hand, and realized she'd tightened her fingers around his, a physical response to her inner ruminations.

A few minutes later, she stood in the living room with Haley's arms wrapped around her neck in a hug while Ches held the little girl. His proximity distracted Grace from Haley and her scent of sweet grass and little girl sweat. Grace's attention wavered to him, saw those beautiful green irises of his eyes watching her steadily. She could feel the warmth of his body standing close to hers, see a small scar below his lip.

"Wish you could stay and tuck me in," Haley said against her.

Grace leaned back and kissed her cheek. "Thank you, little one. I need to get home though."

Haley held onto Grace, nearly pulling her off balance. "When will you come back?"

Ches steadied Grace with one hand, and gently disengaged Haley from her neck with the other. "We'll figure something out. Now, let her go before you make her fall."

Haley loosened her arms, and Ches stepped back breaking the connection among the three of them. Grace moved away as well, her heart thumping hard enough that she wondered if they could hear it. Picking up her purse she'd left on the side table next to the couch, Grace breathed deeply and walked step by step toward the front door, hoping to calm her heart, her nerves, her spirit, every part of her that wanted to stay.

Outside, she opened the car door when Ches' voice stopped her from entering the vehicle.

"Grace?" he called.

Looking behind her, she saw Ches stepping off the front porch.

"Yes?"

He stopped a few feet from her. Grace's fingers tightened around her key ring.

"I just wanted to... thank you for bringing me home. And everything else too."

Grace tilted her face upward. She smiled. "It was the least I could do."

"No, it wasn't." He took a step forward.

"What?"

He reached his hand up, grasping the edge of the door, and Grace was cocooned between the car and him. "It wasn't the least you could do. The least you could do would have been nothing."

Grace focused on the column of his neck. If she looked into his eyes, she'd be lost. She knew it.

Breathe. Breathe. Breathe.

"It seemed providential that you ended up at my hospital. Doing nothing never occurred to me. Besides, I owed you. Helping a stranded woman in the ditch, lending aid, the wedding, all of that."

Ches didn't speak. Grace finally met his gaze.

Oh, my. He was close.

"All of that," he said. He cradled her face, and bending down he kissed her forehead, in a touch that was so soft and sweet, Grace felt tears sting her eyes.

Then he was walking away in long strides, to the porch, in the house, and the door shut behind him. Grace collapsed on the seat, and with a shaky hand, she pulled the car door, hearing it click closing herself inside. Somehow she inserted the key in the ignition and turned it.

This is silly. He kissed my forehead. Not even a kiss, really. A gesture of gratitude. That's all it was.

****

Grace walked out of the hospital and blinked in the late afternoon sunlight. Reaching into her purse, she retrieved her cell phone and looked at the screen as she paused at the crosswalk in the parking lot.

Missed call from…oh…Ches, and a voice mail.

Hmm.

She chose the icon to listen to the message and placed the phone to her ear.

"Hi. It's Ches. I wanted to make good on our date. Wondering if you are free Friday night." He paused. "I'll try not to have a heart attack this time. Call me. Will you?"

A smile broke on Grace's face. He had called her! He wanted to go out with her. Yay!

She waited until she entered her car and had the engine running with the air conditioner running to cool the interior before she called him back.

He picked up after two rings. "Hi, Sugar."

Grace's toes curled at the sound of his smooth voice in

her ear. "Hi."

"Did you listen to my message?"

"Yes. I'm free Friday night. What time shall I come over?"

"Tell you what. Let me come to you. We'll have a nice dinner and go to a show."

"A show?"

"Yeah. I saw there's a play at the Blue Theater. It's not exactly paint-drying, but it's about as close to culture as I can come up with. That suit you?"

"Yes."

The Blue, a charming theater in the downtown district, catered to the elite and artistic crowd. Several of their original productions had won prestigious awards making the theater a cultural attraction for tourists and locals alike.

Grace would have to dress up, and so would Ches.

If possible, her smile widened.

Maybe he'd wear his nice boots again.

Friday evening, Grace's doorbell chimed. She glanced at the clock. Six on the dot. He was prompt. Smoothing her skirt as she walked to the door, she opened it.

There stood Ches in a crisp ebony button down shirt and pants with a razor thin crease down the front. No boots this time. At least not cowboy boots, coal leather Chukka boots completed the ensemble.

They matched, for Grace, too, had chosen a midnight colored flowy dress that ended at the knee, and two inch heels. She'd bought them especially for the date, the first time she'd ever chosen shoes with a heel, always reluctant before to add height to her stature. But tonight she didn't have to worry about towering over her date. Ches was still three inches above her.

He smiled and bent his head forward in greeting, keeping eye contact with her. "Evenin', ma'am."

Grace's heart thumped in her chest. Every woman. Every single woman on this earth ought to have a man greet her this way.

"Would you like to come inside?" she asked.

Ches shook his head. "We probably should go. I made a 6:30 reservation at the restaurant."

Grace smiled. "So, not fast food?"

His eyes crinkled in a returning grin. "Not tonight."

Grace walked over and picked up her purse. Ches stepped over the threshold, eyeing the rocking chair where her purse had been sitting.

He ran his hand over the carved back. "This is beautiful."

"Thanks. My granddaddy made it."

Ches bent and peered at the inlaid turtles Granddaddy had crafted in the carved wood. "Do you like turtles?"

"My granddaddy does. He always puts turtles on the rocking chairs he makes."

"How come?"

She looked at the beautiful design on the chair. It had been her grandparents' gift to her on her thirtieth birthday, a message to her, she suspected. But whether the message was a subtle hint she was turning into an old maid, or their hope for her that she would enjoy many more years, she'd never been sure.

She shouldered her bag and stepped to the door. "Turtles symbolize long life."

Ches followed her. They walked to his truck, and he opened the passenger side door. Taking her hand, he guided her inside. Grace noted Haley's car seat was missing, and the interior gleamed—not even a stray napkin on the floorboard.

He cleaned his truck for me.

The thought sent tingles up her arms and neck.

In a moment, he was beside her in the cab. Just the two of them. No five-year-old chaperone chattering about anything which came into her head. No small body in the car seat situated between them. A new wave of tingles coursed through her. Ches placed his arm on the back of the bench seat and turned his head over his shoulder to back the vehicle out of the driveway.

The warmth of his arm against her shoulder hitched

her breath. She stole a glance at him. No hint of beard. He must have shaved this afternoon. Another clue he'd taken special care for their date.

"So, all his rocking chairs have five turtles?"

"No. Each chair is different. Granny's has two turtles in the middle with tiny turtles around the edge. My mom's chair has three turtles: two big ones, and a baby one in the middle. He gave it to her on her thirtieth birthday. She was pregnant with me at the time."

He removed his arm and shifted gears maneuvering the truck on the road toward downtown. "Huh. How long have you had your chair?"

"Two years."

"Do you have kids I don't know about?"

Grace snickered. "There may be a message in the turtles, but I never asked. We'll just leave it at a blessing for a long life."

Dinner was Italian in a cozy restaurant with low lighting and a guitarist playing in the corner, an oversized brandy glass on a small table beside him. Though Grace had heard of the restaurant and driven by it dozens of times, she'd never come here.

It was definitely a venue for a date night.

Ches pulled her chair from the table and waited for her to sit. When she looked at the menu, she blinked. There were no prices on anything. Her gaze met Ches' over the menu.

"What's wrong?"

"I don't know how much anything costs," she replied.

His lips parted in a grin. "Want to switch?"

No way. The restaurant had gender specific menus? "You're kidding. That seems bold in this day and age."

He shrugged, seeming to be amused by her response. "Me holding the door for you might have been a giveaway. We can ask for another menu, if you want. But I really do want to pay for the meal and the show. Seeing as it's my birthday celebration, and I should get my wish to take a lady out for a good time."

"I thought you didn't want to celebrate your birthday."

A bit of the light dimmed in his gaze. "I don't. Will you let me buy you dinner and take you to the theater?"

The waiter approached. "Are you ready to order, or do you need a few more minutes?" he said.

Ches watched her, waiting.

She wished she knew how much the meals were. She didn't want to order anything expensive. She chose a dish she assumed was on the lower end of the scale with a house salad and offered the menu to the waiter. Ches chose a steak and shrimp combination, a dish, Grace suspected was not cheap.

"Are you sure you don't want to change your mind, sugar?" he asked. "I've heard the steak here is mighty good."

She shook her head.

Ches surrendered his menu, and the waiter left. "If you like, you can try mine. I ordered enough to share."

"Perhaps." Grace sat back. "May I ask a personal question?"

"I suppose."

"Are you taking your medicine?"

Ches arched an eyebrow. "It's going to be that way, is it?"

"You were so adamant in the hospital. I wonder if you've made peace that you're human and that you need to stay healthy."

He didn't answer for a moment. Grace decided he wasn't going to answer at all. Then, "Yes, I'm taking the medicine."

He was holding something back. What was he not telling her?

"But?"

He bent his head, breaking eye contact. "But ultimately, it won't change anything."

"It already has changed. Don't you see? You didn't die."

He met her gaze again, this time not speaking.

"You said all of the males in your family have died before 40. But you survived. You've already broken the pattern."

"I'm not 40 yet."

"This is true, but didn't you tell me your dad and granddad died of massive heart attacks?"

"Yes."

"Did either of them have heart problems before they died?"

"No. No warning. No issues at all."

Grace smiled triumphantly. "See? You've broken the pattern. You survived your heart attack. They didn't."

"Maybe so, Sugar. But I'm not 40 yet. Have you ever been to The Blue?"

Grace studied him. "You don't want to talk about it anymore."

"Nope."

Grace straightened her shoulders. She'd let it go.

For now.

The conversation moved to lighter topics. By the time they sat in The Blue with only the aisle lanterns lit and the stage awash with entertainment, Grace had relaxed, enjoying Ches' charm and the feel of his hand around hers.

After the show, they walked with clasped hands to his truck. He opened the door for her, and after she settled on the seat, he paused, watching her in the darkened interior.

Grace returned his look, and instead of the anticipation of a kiss, she saw instead sadness.

She recognized the expression. She'd seen it many times in patients who had just been told they had cancer or some other life threatening illness, patients who believed there was no treatment available to beat the disease, patients who had been given a death sentence.

She reached and grasped his hand.

"Ches," she murmured.

"Yes, sugar?"

"I want to go out with you again. Next week. I'll come to your house, or you and the girls can come to mine."

"No," he whispered.

Grace leaned toward him. "You're not going to die soon." She didn't even try to keep the vehemence out of her voice. "You're going to live to be old. There's no reason to think otherwise as long as you do what the doctor said."

"You can't fight gen—"

Grace shot up, aimed her mouth on his, wrapped her arms around the breadth of his shoulders, and shut up his hopeless, desolate, determination to die before 40 no matter what.

She drew back, but his arms enclosed her. Opening her eyes, she saw the desolation was gone, replaced by appreciation.

Perhaps even a glimmer of humor.

"Is this how you win an argument?" His arms tightened a fraction.

"Did I win?"

He bent his head and kissed her briefly. Smiling, he released her, and she slid back into the seat. "I can't for the life of me remember what we were arguing about."

Grace remembered. After Ches closed the door and began walking around the truck, she located her cell phone in her purse and made a phone call. When she said goodbye and pressed the end button, Ches started the engine.

"Is everything all right?" he asked.

"Yes, but do you mind if we go somewhere before you take me home?"

"No, I don't mind." His answer held a curious tone, but Grace did not disclose why they were making an expected stop, only directions to get there.

In twenty minutes, Ches steered into the parking lot of a large wraparound building.

"This is nice. What is it?"

"It's a retirement village."

Ches chuckled. "Why did I think you were taking me somewhere so we could make out?"

Grace smiled before opening the door and exiting the

vehicle. Ches met her next to the truck, and she took his hand. "Come on."

"What are we doing exactly?"

She led him past a fountain with a metal sculpture of an elderly man pushing an elderly woman in a swing, their carved faces full of delight. "You'll see."

Ches' gaze roved over the art piece. "What kind of message is this for old people? Someone is going to break a hip."

Grace loved the fountain and the sculpture. "The message is you're never too old to enjoy living."

"Is this what you wanted to show me?"

Grace nudged him affectionately with her shoulder. "Why? Does it make you change your mind about dying?"

Ches sighed. "It's not about changing my mind. Heart disease runs in my family. I can't change that no matter how hard I think."

They entered the lobby, a spacious carpeted room with sofas, easy chairs, and several end tables filled with knickknacks giving the room a homey atmosphere. A man rose from behind a marble table.

"Hi, can I... oh, hi, Grace. How are you?" He reached forward and shook Grace's hand.

"I'm fine, Reuben. This is my friend Ches."

Reuben shook Ches' hand as well, smiling at him. "Hello, sir. You all here to see Homer and Brenda?"

"Yes. I've called, and they're still up."

"Great."

Grace bent over the table and picking up a pen, she wrote their names in the visitors' notebook and filled in the date and time.

Straightening, she guided Ches through the room and down a hallway. They came to an alcove with a giant fish tank. She turned left and knocked on a closed door.

"Who are Homer and Brenda?" Ches asked.

"My grandparents. I moved to Carlton to be closer to them."

A summons to enter reached her, and Grace opened

the door and walked in. Meemee sat on her rocking chair and Grandpa was in his wheelchair in their living room, one of two rooms they lived in now. Grace kissed and hugged each one before introducing them to Ches.

"Y'all have a seat," Meemee said. "You want some water or coke? If I had known you were coming sooner, I could have ordered some tea."

"We're fine." Grace sat on the couch and patted the cushion next to her, giving Ches a warm glance to join her.

"What're you selling?" Grandpa asked.

Brenda leaned toward him. "It's Grace, your granddaughter. She's not selling anything. She came by for a visit."

His forehead wrinkled in thought. "Huh."

Brenda smiled as if Homer had made a joke.

"I'll probably run by the store tomorrow. Do you need me to pick anything up for you?" Grace asked.

"Oh, that'd be nice." The woman pushed herself from the chair and walked to a roll topped desk in the corner. She opened a drawer and withdrew a paper. "Just a few things, if you please." Holding out her hand, she gave the paper to Grace who looked over the items.

"So, Ches, is it? What do you do?"

"I farm in the warm months and run an ash truck in the county in the cold ones."

He did? Grace studied him. He cast her a sidelong glance and shrugged, as if saying 'you never asked.'

"Really? I didn't know we had any farms around here."

"He lives in Wren's Holler, Meemee."

"You got any soap?" Homer asked. "The kind for poison ivy."

"She doesn't have any soap," Brenda said to him.

"Are you getting any in?" he asked Grace. "We'll take a gross."

"Now what do we need with a gross of poison ivy soap, Homer?"

"Gal's got to make a living."

"Yes, she does." Brenda reached over and squeezed

the elderly man's hand. Ches' sharp intake of breath captured Grace's attention. His narrowed eyes focused on the couple, and though he was polite when Meemee asked him a question, he kept his answers concise and short.

Grace stood and kissed her grandparents. "We better go. It's late. Grandpa, I'll bring you some soap when I come back. Anything else you want?"

"Number four sandpaper if you have it."

"All right."

"Got some birdhouses I need to finish up."

As they walked to Ches' truck, Grace wondered if coming here had been a mistake. She had hoped meeting her grandparents would give him hope that he, too, could have a long life. That not everyone dies young.

"Does he still do woodwork?"

"Small projects, yes. Mainly because Meemee won't let him use the more dangerous tools and he doesn't have any place to work anymore."

"What was that about the soap?"

"Sometimes he doesn't remember me. I look familiar, but he can't place me. I think he thinks I sell things because I often bring groceries to their apartment."

"Doesn't it bother you that he doesn't know you?"

Grace smiled. "I know him. He's my grandpa, and I love him. That's what matters."

"It seems...." Ches stopped and shook his head. "a lot for your grandmother to have to handle. Him being in a wheelchair and....being confused."

"That's why they moved here, so he can get the help he needs. Meemee won't ever leave him. They've been married 61 years. Here they can still live together, but there's a nurse on the floor and staff to take care of what Meemee can't do. They eat in the dining room. It's a really nice place."

Ches opened the door of the truck. He held her hand and guided her inside. He stood there and made sure she was settled before he shut the door. The silence in the cab as Ches drove back to Grace's house gave her time to appreciate his attentiveness and his gentlemanly manners. She wondered if he'd walk her to her front porch and if he'd kiss her goodnight.

Should she invite him in, and if she did, would he expect more than a goodnight kiss?

Her forward behavior in the parking lot might have given him the wrong signal.

Grace shifted in the seat. It had been so long since she'd been on a date. She hated the uncertainty, of not knowing Ches' intentions, of not wanting to disappoint him, of not wanting to be disappointed by him.

When her house came into view, Ches slowed the truck and turned into her driveway. He shifted in park, but didn't cut the engine.

Grace risked a glance at him and noted his profile illuminated by the dashboard light.

"Thanks for a nice time." She pressed the handle of the door, but before she could exit the vehicle, he was there standing beside her.

Butterflies took flight in her stomach, and she folded her arms over her midriff in attempt to quell them. The door loomed, and Grace reached into her purse for the key, but it wasn't in the pocket where she normally kept it. She felt in another compartment wishing she'd turned on the porch light.

This is silly. It's not like I haven't kissed him already.

"Sugar?"

Grace paused in her search. Ches' expression was hard to read in the dark.

"I had a nice time tonight, too. And I'd like to take you up on your invitation for another date, if that invitation is still on the table."

Happy, Grace put her arms around him and hugged him. His arms wound around her, cocooning her in the warmth of his much larger frame. He chuckled and kissed the top of her head.

"I suppose that means it's still on the table."

"Sure." Grace lay her head in the crook of his neck for

a moment. In the quiet she could hear his heart beating.

She closed her eyes. *Thank you, Lord, for tall men, specifically for this one holding me right now.*

She stepped away from him, but captured his hand in hers. "Where do you want to go?"

"Come over to the house. I'll cook. Maybe I can talk Sunni into making an appearance this time."

"How about I bring over my mom's chicken casserole, and you provide the rest?"

He grinned. "What goes with your mom's chicken casserole? Peas and carrots, I suppose."

Chapter Eight

The next day, Grace's mother called her.

Obviously Meemee had told her about Grace and Ches' visit the night before.

"I suppose you know why I'm calling. Is everyone in the family going to get to meet Ches before me and your father?"

Grace smiled. "What can I say, Mom? They're closer than you are."

"So, is it getting serious?"

Grace turned that question over in her mind. She chose her words carefully. "Ches is a good man, Mom."

"Of course, he is. Otherwise, you wouldn't be avoiding my question."

Penny had always been very perceptive.

"Do you love him?"

Grace huffed. "Come on, Mom. I barely know him."

"That's not what I asked."

Did she? Grace's throat closed, making it hard to speak. "I... I like him a lot, Mom. But he's got some things going on in his life right now."

"Oh." Penny didn't speak for a moment. "Has he told you what these things are?"

"He didn't have to. He missed our first date because he had a heart attack. He's only 39, so it really threw him for a loop."

"Well, of course it would. He's probably scared out of his mind."

Grace didn't reply.

"Is he okay now? His heart, I mean?"

"I hope so. He's not been sick before this, so taking medicine is something he's never done, and he doesn't like that."

"You can encourage him, though, to take care of himself."

Grace remembered the confrontation in his hospital

room when she'd threatened to shove the pills down his throat. He'd said she'd put the fear of Grace into him. Her skin warmed in embarrassment at the memory.

"So, when you went over to your dad's parents, was that your first date?"

"Yes. I was hoping if he met Meemee and Grandaddy, he'd see some people live beyond 40."

"Hmm. Did you convince him?"

"I don't know, Mom. He's sort of an ongoing project."

"Really? He's a project to you?"

Grace squeezed her eyes shut. Her heart pumped heavily, responding to the overwhelming emotion of knowing Chesapeake Larson wasn't just a project to her.

"And he's very tall. Something I'm sure you really like about him."

"Yes." Mom had made self-effacing comments during Grace's teenage years, blaming herself for Grace's stature because Penny, too, was unusually tall. Until one day, Grace said firmly to her to stop blaming herself because she didn't control her own height or anyone else's, and if God had meant them to be over six feet, then that was fine, because God knew what he was doing. Mom had never brought it up again.

"Well." Grace's father and mother were exactly the same height. Six, one. "I never did find someone taller than I was. But then again, once I met your dad, I quit looking."

I think I'm falling in love with him.

Grace almost said the words, but she didn't. She hadn't ever been in love before. What did it feel like? Thinking about him at different times of the day and night. Her heart hammering when she remembered his voice calling her *Sugar* or *Miss Grace*. Or when he said, *Yes ma'am.* When the image of his face—how his eyes crinkled at the corners and the curve of his mouth when he smiled—filled her mind. And when they'd kissed. They'd actually kissed! Oh, my gosh, the intensity of those feelings made her stomach quiver.

Almost like she was going to throw up.

"Honestly." Grace laughed. "I get sick to my stomach sometimes when I think about him. Weird, huh?"

"Oh, dear me. It's like that, is it?"

"He is such a kind and good man. I really like him."

"I'm glad, Grace. I'm glad you've found someone you really like."

Grace hoped Ches felt the same way.

****

Tuesday morning found Grace at the hospital. She remembered Ches had a follow up appointment with Dr. Akeem this week and decided to call to see if he would meet her for lunch after the doctor's visit.

He picked up on the first ring. "Hey, Sugar."

Grace grinned at the endearment. "Do you always answer your phone that way?"

"Nope."

"How come you call me Sugar?"

"Cause you were sweet to my little girl. I appreciate that in a woman."

"Even before I spoke to Haley, you nicknamed me that. In fact, it was the first word you ever spoke to me."

"Really?" His tone indicated he was teasing her.

"Yes."

"When a woman is stranded on the side of the road nursing a cut foot, it seems to me a little sweet talk thrown her way couldn't hurt."

"So, 'sugar' is a term you use whenever you come upon a woman in need?"

"I might call her that before I know her name, but as I said, you were sweet to my little girl. You've earned the title." He paused, and a note of hesitation entered his voice. "You don't mind me calling you that, do you?"

"Nope."

Ches laughed. "Did you have a reason for calling?"

"I was wondering if you've already had your doctor's appointment. I remembered it was ten in the morning, but couldn't recall what day."

Silence met her comment.

"Ches?"

"Hmm?"

"Your follow up appointment with Dr. Akeem. Is it today?"

"Nope."

"When is it?"

"It... *was* today, but I cancelled it."

Disappointment filled her chest. She had hoped she wouldn't have to wait until Saturday night to see him again. "When's the rescheduled appointment?"

Ches' sigh filled her ears.

Oh. So, he hadn't rescheduled.

"I see," she said. And she did. He had canceled the appointment and he had no plans to reschedule it probably because he didn't think Dr. Akeem could do anything to help him.

"Go ahead," Ches said.

Confused, Grace shook her head though she knew Ches couldn't see her. "Go ahead?"

"Yes. Go ahead. Fuss at me. I know you want to."

Yes, she did. But had she earned the right to harangue him about his health? A few kisses didn't give her power to tell him what to do.

Did it?

"Ches, if you take care of yourself. If you take the medication prescribed to you—as it was prescribed—and if you keep your doctor appointments, you have a much better chance of living a long life."

He didn't respond.

Irritation pricked at Grace. "Did you hear me?"

"Yes, I heard you, Sugar." His accommodating tone rankled her further.

"No, you didn't," Grace snapped. "At least you heard me, but you're not listening. Why are you so stubborn? So determined you're going to die?"

"You know, Grace. You work in a hospital. You see people getting better, but in my experience, nothing changes the outcome. We all die. All of us. All the praying in the world won't change a thing."

"How can you know that?"

"Because I prayed that my mother wouldn't die, and I prayed for my father, too. Nobody heard. Nobody listened. And nobody did what I wanted. What I needed. I appreciate that the God thing works for you, and I hope you don't take this the wrong way, but it doesn't for me."

Grace gripped the phone tightly, absorbing the hopelessness in Ches' message. He'd lost both of his parents. He'd prayed, and God hadn't answered his prayers.

"It's not fair, is it, that your mom and dad died so young."

"Nope. But life isn't fair. I learned that lesson a long time ago."

"I wish I could have known you back then."

"Why? So you could have prayed for them? So, you could have saved my soul and convinced me that the God who killed my parents loves me?"

"No, so I could have wrapped my arms around you and absorbed some of the grief and sadness."

Ches made a sound of disbelief. "You were, what, five when my mother died? What did you know about giving comfort?"

"How do you feel when Haley hugs you? I would have been her age."

"All right, you got me there, but at twelve I doubt I would have appreciated it."

"Of course, you would have. You were very lonely and missing your mother so terribly. I think hugs would have helped you a lot. If you were here, I'd give you one right now."

"I just told you I don't believe in God, and you offer hug therapy. Sugar, I really don't get you."

"The god you don't believe in is the one who always answers prayers the way we want him to. I don't believe in that god either. The God I do believe in is the One you're angry at. He's the One who chased a deer across a country road, so I could meet you. He's the One who guided a scared 19-year-old to call 911 when her dad collapsed in the kitchen. He's the One who engineered the EMTs to take that man to Regional Hospital so I could pray at his bedside and comfort his girls in the waiting room."

"And if you had died swerving to miss the deer?"

"But I didn't die. I got my date, and Haley and Sunni still have you. For now. If you don't change your mind about dying, if you don't start taking better care of that heart of yours, the only thing I can think to do is marry you so I can take care of your girls when you die. But it doesn't have to come to that. Will you please go to your follow up appointment with Dr. Akeem?"

Ches didn't answer. Grace waited. Still nothing.

"Ches?"

"Yeah?"

"The follow up appointment. Will you make one and keep it?"

"I have a farm to run. I don't have time for all these doctor appointments. It's pointless."

"Who will run the farm when you die?"

"I better go. I'll see you, Grace."

Grace held the phone away from her ear and pressed the red 'end' icon, before Ches could disconnect. He had, in effect, ended the call already.

Humiliation blanketed her. How could she be so dumb! She'd come across like a steamroller, telling him how he ought to live his life, bullying him about going to the doctor, where he went wrong in grieving his parents, what was wrong with him.

What was wrong with him, ha! What was wrong with her? Grace wanted to be his girlfriend, not baby him as if she were his mother.

Why had she pushed him so, sticking her nose in his business as if she had the right.

Even though, not taking care of himself could mean that Haley and Sunni wouldn't have him around. What would they do without him?

He was a grown man. Surely he knew not following up

with the doctor and not taking his medicine could mean severe consequences.

Why? Why was he being so stubborn about it? Just because his father and grandfather had died at 39 didn't mean he would. Especially if he made better decisions about his health.

She should have treaded more carefully with him about his health and about the unresolved spiritual grief he still harbored. Yes, he had brought up unanswered prayer and God, but she hadn't used it as an opening to shame him.

Had she?

Grace replayed their conversation in her mind.

Ches had brought up God more than once. Maybe he wanted to talk about it. Or maybe he was uncomfortable knowing she was a woman of faith, and he wanted to be clear with her where he stood. Could that be it?

Whether it was or wasn't, Grace had been clear right back.

She didn't want to force her beliefs on him, but she also didn't want him to make assumptions about her own faith.

She had come into Ches' life for a reason.

Perhaps the reason was so she could help him come to his own decision to take care of himself. She wanted to fight for him. To fight alongside him. But not against him.

Why hadn't she let it go on the phone?

And how could she convince him that if he took care of himself, he didn't have to die before 40?

****

The next day at the hospital, Grace received a call alerting her to go to the emergency department. An infant, unresponsive, had come in by ambulance. Grace sat with the parents in the conference room while the staff worked to save the baby's life. Several times she went back to check on the status and found the team of nurses and doctors performing CPR.

After 40 almost minutes without regaining a heartbeat, the doctor called it.

Jennifer Johnson

The baby died.

In such cases, the police interviewed the family as part of an investigation as to whether they were culpable in the death. The whole process, though necessary, was gut-wrenching. Grace stayed with the parents as a support and offered what comfort she could.

It was always the most difficult work because not only were the parents grieving their baby, but they often felt they were being accused of harming the child, though it was protocol to investigate any death that happened in someone's home.

Sad, too, was most of the time an autopsy had to be performed on the baby, so the parents would leave the hospital, devastated and in shock. And their child would go to Columbus in a body bag.

A little one.

Grace walked with Emily and Robert, the baby's parents, to the lobby. Emily clutched a package to her chest. It contained hand and foot prints of Mia, their six-week-old daughter. Grace had called Rusty, a pediatric nurse to press the infant's hand and foot in soft clay encased in small pads. It was meant as a keepsake of their child whom they had lost, a little comfort in what was likely the worst day of their lives.

In the lobby Grace hugged Emily, the corner of the box of Mia's prints pressing into her chest, a reminder of the chasm of her absence.

"You take care, okay?" Grace said against the other woman's hair. She wished she could make it better, fix it, help it. But there was nothing. Nothing that could make this okay.

Grace had been a chaplain long enough to accept that truth.

She stepped away from the couple. Robert put his arm around his wife and, bent from grief, they walked to the glass doors of the entrance of the hospital.

Grace watched them go, and then turned and ascended the staircase to the small chapel. She sat inside the quiet room and closed her eyes. No words came to her to pray. The raw emotion of the morning still whipped at her.

She breathed in through her nostrils, counting to four, then kept the breath to the count of seven, then slowly released it to eight. The mindfulness exercise calmed the traumatic voices of unfairness and sadness.

She repeated the breathing several times until a one-word prayer entered her mind.

Please.

It echoed in the blank recesses of her spent emotions.

Please. Please. Please.

She wasn't even sure what she was pleading for. God knew. That was enough.

She rose from the chair and left the quiet sanctuary. The waiting room outside of the chapel, reserved for outpatient registration, usually had several people seated at the perimeter. A man occupying one of the chairs stood capturing Grace's attention.

She inhaled in recognition.

"Hey," Ches said. Dressed in blue jeans and a white T-shirt and the boots he had worn the day she met him, he held a ratty baseball hat in his hands.

What was he doing here?

"I…uh…." The corner of his mouth sloped north, and a crease appeared in his cheek. "I came to get my hug."

A sob wrenched itself from her mouth, and she clasped her hand over her lips to keep any more from escaping. Ches' expression changed from uncertainty to concern. In two strides he was in front of her.

"What is it, Sugar?" he said.

Grace shook her head. "I can't," she whispered brokenly. "I can't give any hugs right now. I can only receive them."

"All right." He enfolded her in his arms, the familiar scent of outdoors and the cologne he must use surrounded her, that and the warmth and strength of his frame.

Realizing she was crying, she sniffed and drew back. His arms fell away from her. Staring at his shirt collar, she spoke. "Thank you."

"Yep."

Another sob escaped, this one twirled together with a chuckle. She could really learn to love this man.

She stepped backward, twice, three times. It did little to quell the overwhelming urge to bury herself in another embrace.

As good as the moment felt in Chesapeake Larson's arms, he couldn't fix what was wrong either. In fact, he himself wrestled with similar feelings of grief and sadness which had yet to be resolved though his parents had been gone many years.

"Would you like to go to lunch?" Grace said.

"Are you hungry?"

She shook her head. The turmoil of the morning robbed her appetite.

"Then let's get something to drink and find a quiet place to visit. Are there any places like that around here?"

Grace showed him to the cafeteria, all without words.

With bottles of water in hand, Grace led him to her office, a modest room dominated by corner desk. She grasped the back of the desk chair and positioned it to face the only other chair in the room.

"How did you know where I was?" Grace asked after they were seated.

"I saw you go in there."

The chapel. He hadn't joined her because, in his own words, the God thing didn't work for him. Instead of asking him the question she already knew the answer to, she remained silent.

"Who was that couple?" Ches asked.

Robert and Emily. He must have seen her with them.

"They are." Grace took a shuddering breath. "were parents of a patient."

Ches' gaze fell from hers. He had caught the change in verb tense and realized what it meant. "How old was their child?"

"Two months."

He shook his head and rested his elbows on his thighs. "What do you say to that?"

"There's not much that can be said."

A long silence followed. Finally, Ches met her eyes. "How can you be okay with it?"

"I'm not."

"You still believe in God after he took their baby? What kind of God does that, Grace?"

A tear fell from Grace's eye. "He didn't."

Ches straightened. "He didn't stop it," he countered.

"No."

If her time as a hospital chaplain had taught her anything, it was that life and death happened with little correlation with what she considered fair. She had to believe that God understood, even when she didn't.

"Then what's the point of praying, believing, if life is still going to kick you in the teeth?"

"Because at least I know I'm not alone. Someone bigger than me knows. Someone who loves me."

Ches shook his head. "What good is the love if it doesn't change the outcome?"

"Love makes a difference. It always makes a difference." If Grace knew anything, she knew that.

His vivid green eyes glittered with intensity. "Why does it make a difference? Why does it matter? The baby still died."

Grace closed her eyes. Yes, the baby still died. The sadness of it blanketed her again. She breathed in and out. Felt the peace of an answer coming to her. Opening her eyes, she met Ches' hard gaze. "Because I believe in a place where the baby doesn't stay dead. I believe in a place where there is no more pain, and I believe in God who understands even when I don't. Those things give me hope to keep going."

"What if you're wrong?" he asked.

"What if you are?"

After a minute, Ches shrugged his shoulders. Grace slumped. "Good. Does that mean you're done making me think hard things? I've had a difficult day. I'm ready for a break."

Ches smiled. "Sugar, you're pretty good at thinking hard things. Much better than me."

"You know what I'd like?"

"What?"

"Something chocolate. Want to see if they have anything in the vending machine? We can split it."

Ches' brows lowered in disapproval. "Vending machine candy? Don't they have dessert in the cafeteria?"

"You don't like candy bars?" She opened a drawer and rummaged through her purse, picking out quarters from her wallet.

"Well, yeah, but I'm not so sure about splitting one with you. First you propose marriage, then you want to share a meager portion of a sweet. You move mighty fast, sugar."

Grace stood and walked to the door. She glanced over her shoulder at him. "Seems like a man who thinks he's going to be dead within a year would want to move fast."

"Better watch out. I might just call your bluff."

****

Haley squealed. Grace didn't let it distract her. She kept her attention on the bean bags she tossed in the air in the Larson living room. Ches sat on the couch and Haley had been sitting next to him until the excitement of Grace's juggling had propelled her to her feet like a jumping bean. Sunni sat cross-legged on the floor near the fireplace with Jojo's head resting on her knee. The young woman hadn't moved from the spot since Grace arrived a half hour ago, but her presence suggested she and Ches had arrived at some sort of peace agreement.

"Please, Miss Grace! Teach me how to do that," Haley begged.

One. Two. Three. Grace let the balls fall into her hand before she spoke. "All right. Come here." In a second, Haley was in front of her. Grace turned her around and placed the balls in her hand. "Start with these two in one

hand. And you throw one up and practice catching it."
Haley threw it high enough that it hit the ceiling. Grace
lunged, but it was too far, though Ches reached his hand
out and caught it.

"Good catch, Pop," Grace said.

Ches' eyebrow arched. "Back at cha." He tossed it, and
Grace caught the beanbag.

"Gently, sweetheart. Only about this high because you
want to be able to catch it without moving your feet."
Grace demonstrated.

Haley threw the bag, but it fell to the floor. She picked
it up and attempted again. After several tries, Grace said,
"Perhaps you should start with just one beanbag."

"Just one?"

"Work on tossing... That's good, but that's more like
throwing it. Not so high. Better, then when you can do
that, we'll try two again."

Haley threw the beanbag and it fell to the ground.
Each time she picked it up, never giving up.

"You know, if you stand next to the couch, you won't
have to bend over every time to pick it up," Grace advised.

"Or I can start catching it," Haley replied.

"Yes, or that."

Ches stood. "I'm going to check on supper. Don't
have too much fun without me."

"We won't," Haley said already positioning herself in
front of the spot Ches had vacated.

"She's too little to do it," Sunni said. "All you're going
to do is frustrate her."

"I'm not too little. I can do it," Haley defended. "Can't
I do it, Pop?" She raised her voice to be heard by Ches who
was now in the other room.

"Can you do what?" His call came without an
appearance.

"Can I juggle like Miss Grace?"

A drawer opened then shut. "If you practice a lot," he
replied.

"I'll show you, Sissy. I'll do it."

Sunni arched her eyebrow at the girl, but didn't speak. She unfolded her legs, rising from the floor and left the room, going into the kitchen. Grace heard her speak, and Ches respond. Several exchanges followed, then a door slammed.

Haley continued to throw the beanbag up and continued not to catch it. Sometimes it landed on the couch; sometimes it landed on the floor, the end table, or the recliner. Grace offered bits of advice and repeated it. Soon, Ches called them into the kitchen to eat.

Sunni didn't join them, and there was no empty plate at the table testifying that she would. What was going on with her and Ches?

Neither Ches nor Haley acted as if anything were amiss that Sunni was absent. Was it because she rarely joined them for supper? Twice now, Grace had eaten with them, and twice now, Sunni was a no show.

After supper, Sunni appeared in the kitchen where Ches and Haley washed dishes while Grace dried them with a towel.

"I'll take Little Bit outside for a while," Sunni said. "The lightning bugs are out."

Haley was already moving away from the sink. "I love that idea, Sissy. Pop, we got any empty jars?"

Ches cut his eyes to Grace with a sly smile. "There are some canning jars over the dryer."

"You can food?"

"Have to. We can't eat all the squash and okra since it all comes in at the same time, and since everybody grows it around here, you can't give it away."

"Is there anything you can't do, Chesapeake Larson?"

The door closed behind Sunni and Haley.

"Raising girls, according to my daughter."

"The problem is they don't come with a manual."

"Nope."

Grace waited for him to say more, but he didn't. They finished the dishes in silence. Later, Grace sat on a wooden bench suspended by chains from the ceiling of Ches' massive back porch. Ches settled on the swing as well, but the Haley-sized space between them testified the child had claimed the spot to show them the lightning bugs she had captured before Sunni had taken her and Jojo on a walk. Ches' denim-clad legs stretched out in front of him, anchoring the swing. Though they hadn't spoken since the girls left, sounds of life in the country filled the evening air: A rising and falling chorus of insects, croaking that may have been frogs, the soothing back and forth squeak of the swing chain, and the lowing of cows.

"Do you have cattle?"

"Yep."

"I thought you were a farmer."

"I grow the corn to feed the cattle. Good money in hormone-free, corn-fed beef, so that's what I do. Little more labor-intensive, but it's worth it."

Grace glanced side-long at him. "It doesn't smell like there are cows here."

Ches chuckled. "Wait till it rains."

"Where are they?"

Ches shifted and looked out to where his backyard ended in a fence and beyond high corn plants. "The south and east acreage are the pastures this year. Every three years, I shift the corn and the cows. That way the soil stays fertile without as much fertilizer."

"Ahh. I guess that's why you need a fence. It's not to keep the corn out."

"No ma'am. The fence is for the cows on the years they're in the west pasture, which is that one you see. In the outlying areas I use barbed wire, but the wood fence looks nicer this close to the house. It runs the perimeter of the yard to the road."

Grace didn't reply, taking in the information. The peace of the evening surrounded her like the folds of a handmade quilt.

Grace felt a tickle at her neck and realized Ches was twirling a strand of her hair around his finger. He gave her a self-deprecating smile. "I believe this is the first time I've seen your hair unbound. It's longer than I imagined."

"Than you imagined? Really? You imagined my hair?" She said in a skeptical tone.

"Why, sure I did. Isn't that why ladies put it up, so we'll wonder what they'd look like without all the pins and barrettes?"

"I put it up so it's out of my way."

"Why in the world would...." Ches stopped and crooked his head.

Grace heard a dog barking, but that was it.

"What is it?" Grace asked.

"I thought I heard—"

"Daddy! Daddy!" Sunni's panicked voice reached them. Ches shot out of the swing and ran toward his daughter's call.

And the pond beyond the garage and the barn.

Grace followed him, sprinting as quickly as she could, but not catching up with him. She reached the pond in time to see Sunni standing at the dock and Ches jump in the water.

Haley. She must be in the water.

Sunni screamed her name and paced frantically. "Daddy, hurry!"

Chapter Nine

Grace pumped her legs, hitting the dock with her heeled shoes. Pound. Pound. Pound. She reached the end of the wooden aperture and saw Haley flailing in the water, her small face terror-stricken. Ches was next to her. She latched onto him and climbed on top of him, pushing him beneath the surface.

"Haley, no!" Grace yelled. She dropped to her knees, then collapsed on her stomach, reaching her arm over the side of the last board. "Haley! Grab my hand, baby. Haley!" Grace turned her head. "Sunni! Get behind me and crouch down. I might need you to sit on my legs and anchor me. Be ready."

"Help—me—Poppy," Haley panted.

Ches hadn't surfaced. Graced took a calming breath. "Haley. Little Bit." She reached her arm further. "Take my hand, sweetie."

"I can't. I can't."

"You can. It's all right. You can. Sunni! Don't you think she can do it?"

"Yeah," Sunni said brokenly. "I know you can. Take Grace's hand, Little Bit."

"I'm scared!" she screamed and took in a mouth full of water, beginning to sink.

Grace pushed out as far as possible, grabbed her arm, catching her wrist. She wrenched the girl up, uttering a guttural cry as she used all of her strength to pull Haley up on the dock, throw her over her body to Sunni, and push herself over the edge of the dock into the water to get Ches.

The water was cold, a contrast to the still warm evening. And it was murky. Going straight down, her mind screamed: *Too deep! Too dark! You'll never find him!*

I will. Yes, I will. I will find Ches.

Down further she went, and her hand encountered something, no someone. Completely, still. Grace's mind tamped down what that might mean. She groped in the muddy depth. Head. Arm. Torso. Fishing her hand under his arm, she locked hers around his chest in a hold she'd learned as a lifeguard in high school, crouched her knees and braced her feet on the bottom, then propelled them both upward. She kept her arm like a vice, expecting him to begin thrashing once they hit the surface. They broke into the air—blessed oxygen—she gasped it in, and thank God, thank God, he heaved a breath and began coughing. Other than the spasms of releasing the water from his lungs, he didn't fight, didn't struggle.

Grace bypassed the dock and kicked, swimming for the shore. She touched her foot down, and there it was— soft, slimy, earth. She pivoted both legs, planting her feet— one without her shoe. She kept a hold on Ches, not sure if he were calm enough to stand if she let go. Closer still to shore, she loosened her grip.

"Ches, stand up. We're in shallow water."

Obediently, his weight shifted in the water. She released him, but his arm fastened itself around her shoulders.

"Pop! Pop!"

Grace became aware of Haley's calls and Jojo's barks.

"I'm okay. Okay. Sunni, take her—" His sentence was interrupted by a fit of coughs. "Take her up to the house and get some dry clothes on her and get ready for bed. I'll be up after while."

"But, Daddy—"

"Noooo!"

Both girls protested his order.

"Go on, now. Go on. I'll be up at the house in a bit." They both stood about knee deep in the water. He appeared relaxed, but his arm was heavy on her.

"I don't wanna. Poppy, hold me."

"Sunni, take her and go. Jojo, go with them, boy."

The young woman studied her dad for a couple of seconds, then scooped up Haley and hurried away with the large dog following them. Haley screamed and reached for

Ches. Even when they were out of sight, Haley's wails reached them.

Ches' arm fell, and he sloshed through the water, coughing.

His boots crossed the reeds and rushes at the water's edge, and when he finally stood on land, he collapsed on his hands and knees retching. In a moment, it was over, and he rolled on his back. Grace sat next to him, wringing out her hair and shirt.

"You can't swim, can you?" she asked finally.

His eyes were closed, and his expression relaxed. "Not very well."

"Glad I was here."

He cracked one eye open. Grace noticed an angry red mark at his cheekbone. "Me too."

"What happened to your cheek?"

He touched the spot with his finger. "It's nothing."

Grace leaned toward him for an inspection. "It's something. Did Haley kick you when you jumped in after her?"

"Her elbow, I think." He rose on his elbows and grimaced. "When I think what could have happened...."

"You're not allowed."

Both eyes met hers. "What?"

"You're not allowed to play the what-if game. You'll lose, if you do. Just put it out of your mind."

He crooked his head. "Not so easy to do."

"Focus instead on the here and now. Haley and Sunni are safe. I'm safe. You're safe." Grace paused. "And wet. Your boots—I'm afraid the boots might be the only causality."

"And your shoe."

Grace wiggled her feet and pushed off the other sandal. "Can I tell you something?"

He shrugged. "I suppose."

"When someone is in distress in the water, even if they are not drowning yet, they think they are, and they panic." She made a fist and shook it in front of her. "Fighting for their life, with everything that they are. They will do anything to live, to get out of the water, even climb on top of the person trying to save them. There are people who drowned trying to save someone else because that other person pushed them down and wouldn't let them back up."

She paused and studied his profile, waiting for an acknowledgement of what she was telling him.

"I hear you," he said finally.

"If someone is in the water, jumping in with them is dangerous. The best thing to do is throw a rope, life preserver, or reach a tree branch out even. If you don't have anything like that, you lay down on the edge of the pool or." She pointed. "The dock, and reach your hand out and grab them, but don't let them pull you in or you both could die." She stood and pulled her shirt away from her body. "Come here and let me show you." She took a few steps and looked back at him. He watched her, but she couldn't read his expression. "Come on," she encouraged.

Without a word, he got to his feet and Grace led him to the edge of the floating boards. She sat then lay down on her stomach. "See?" Grace reached her arm over the water.

"But if she's so scared, she won't reach out to the branch or even your hand."

He was talking about Haley, probably remembering her expression of panic above the surface of the pond just before he jumped in after her.

Graced turned on her side and looked up at Ches. From this angle, he was a giant towering over her supine form.

"You are one of the most calm people I've ever met. She knows you. She loves you. She trusts you. You can calm her down enough to reach out to you."

Ches shook his head.

"Yes." Grace sat up. "Yes, Ches."

Though the light was low, she could see the skepticism in his face. She couldn't convince him. She would have to show him.

"Remember, you don't jump in. If you do, you're both

in danger. Reach out and pull her in." She looked out over the water. "How deep is this pond, do you think?"

"Not terribly. 14 feet at its deepest, I think."

Grace imagined 14 feet. Murky. Dark. She bent on the edge of the dock.

"Grace, what are you doing?"

"I want you to pull me out of the water like I showed you." She jumped in, and though she hadn't meant to, her head went below the water. A dark shape moved in front of her. Long and black, she screamed, or attempted to. Instead she took in a mouthful of water. Kicking furiously upward, she sputtered when her head broke water. She was further from the dock then she realized. Ches was already at the edge, crouching.

"There aren't snakes in this pond, are there?"

"Yes," he said calmly, as if it was okay.

"What! I'm scared of snakes."

Ches laughed. "You, Sugar? I didn't think there was anything you were afraid of."

"They're not poisonous at least."

"Just the water moccasins."

"Just the water moccasins? Why do you let Haley come here at all?" Grace stroked toward the dock.

"The snakes are long gone. We've scared them with all of the splashing. He lay down on the boards' edge. "Come on. Take my hand."

Something brushed Grace's foot, and she gasped, moving away from Ches. "Something touched me."

"Grace, darlin', please take my hand."

Grace kicked again, moving closer to him and grabbed his hand with both of hers. Immediately, he pulled hard, and when she was by the dock, he hauled her up, leveraging himself on his knees, then grasping under her arms to get her on his level. She scrambled away from the edge in case any snake might decide to bite her foot.

Ches rose slowly. He placed two fingers in his mouth and let out a sharp whistle, then two more times.

"What are you doing?" she asked.

"You like horses?"

"Sure. Who doesn't?"

He smiled, and one eyebrow lifted. "You ever ridden one?"

"Of course, I have. In the fifth grade at summer camp."

He whistled the same short three tones. "Fifth grade, huh?"

"Why are you asking?"

Then Grace heard it. Him. Galloping coming toward them. She turned, and gasped. A large gray horse ran toward them. He slowed as he neared and stopped at the edge of the dock. Ches met him, and slapped his neck affectionately, then kissed the skin there. "Hey, my Laddie." He turned to Grace. "Come here, and meet Lad."

In the near darkness, the horse appeared the color of violet with black mane and tail. In awe, Grace approached the creature. She and Haley had discussed the definition of the word exquisite. Here was the definition standing majestically before her.

"He's so beautiful," she breathed, reaching up a hand to touch his broad face.

"I think so."

The horse nickered, and Grace laughed.

"You ever ride bareback?"

Grace stepped back, shaking her head. "I'm not riding him. I haven't ridden since I was a child."

"I'll be right here. Come on, now." Ches indicated with his head, she should come closer.

"No. I... I can't."

"Sure, you can. You have no shoes, and I don't want you hurting yourself on the way back to the house. I'll be right here. I'll help you up. It'll be fine."

"Will he... let me?"

"He's a sweetheart. Very well mannered, aren't you, boy?"

The horse moved his head down and up, as if he were nodding.

"You won't let him throw me off?"

"He wouldn't do that, would you, Lad?" He patted the horse's neck.

Grace stood next to Ches and studied the horse, wondering how in the world she would get up on the tall beast.

"If I give you a lift, you think you can get on his back?" Ches asked.

Grace shook her head.

"Yes, you can." He clasped his hands together. "Put your foot in my hands, and I'll heft you up."

Grace studied his hands and the horse. "Left foot?" She put her hands on his shoulder in preparation of the lift.

"Yep."

"Okay." She placed her foot in his hands and hopped, and up she went. Up, up, up. Then she was on top of the horse. "What do I hold onto?"

Ches reached up and touched the hair on Lad's neck. "His mane, but he'll follow me, and I'll guide him. I'll be with you the whole time. You'll be fine, sugar."

Anxiety threatened to engulf her. She could fall off so easily. She leaned forward and gingerly held the long ebony hair.

"Loosen up." Ches put his hand around her calf and shook her leg gently. "And sit tall. You clench your thighs around his body and crouch down, he's going to think you want to go fast."

"You won't let him, Ches!"

He smiled up at her. "I won't, but we don't want to confuse him, do we?"

Lad moved his head to catch a glimpse of Ches, then side-stepped a couple of paces. "Oh!" Panicked by the animal's movement, she looked for something more substantial to hold onto. She didn't want to hurt him by grabbing his mane, but there was nothing else to put her hands on.

Ches walked to the front of the horse, trailing his hand along his beautiful coat as he did so. He stood in front of

Lad who nuzzled him. "Tell me about the good Lord."

"What?"

"The Lord. How you find peace through believing in Him."

Grace searched Ches' face for a challenge or mischief. But she only saw the gentle patience she'd witnessed when he talked to Haley, even when he had enticed her out of the water and away from the snakes.

Grace shivered. She straightened her spine, realizing as she did so, she had hunkered down low over the horse again. "Well, God is with me always. He promised He would be, and I believe him. So...ummm....presence is really important to me. Knowing I'm not alone."

"Is God with you now up there on Lad's back?"

Aha. She saw now what Ches was doing. She smiled at him. "Yes, even way up here without a seatbelt to keep me on. I'm scared, but no matter what, God knows my fear and understands it, and you're here. You trust Lad not to hurt me, and I trust you." Grace closed her eyes briefly and took a deep breath. Opening her eyes, she met Ches' gaze. "I trust you, Ches."

He watched her for a moment. Something passed back and forth between them. Awareness, perhaps, but also an understanding. Grace was offering him a precious gift of herself: trust. She'd asked him to trust her about his own health. She'd seen his vulnerability and attempted to comfort him as a chaplain, as a woman in gratitude for how he had helped her the day they met, and recognition of the potential of something more.

She was falling in love with Chesapeake Larson.

I can't, though, because he doesn't know the Lord. Not really. I need to save my heart for a man of faith.

Grace had known several of her close friends who had fallen in love and married men who had no interest in serving God or even making time in their life for him. Eventually, to keep the peace in the marriage, her friends had let go of their commitment to God. Grace would not do that.

She did trust Ches. And somewhere when she hadn't been paying attention, she'd entrusted her heart to him. But she knew she could not pursue this relationship unless Ches had a change in heart toward the Lord.

Ches is a faithful man. Trust Me to show you. Trust yourself to show him Me.

Oh.

The voice—or whatever it was—stamped that message on her mind and heart.

She believed that Ches was faithful, yes. She knew he was a good and kind man. But could he forgive God for the pain he'd suffered in the past—a mother who he'd lost as a child, a father who had died when Ches was only a young man, a sister who'd killed herself with a drug overdose leaving behind an orphaned baby, and an ex-wife who'd abandoned Ches and Sunni?

Oooh.

With new eyes, Grace gazed at Ches.

Every person from Ches' childhood had gone away, leaving him to care for a daughter and a niece by himself.

Was it any wonder that he felt God had abandoned him too?

Here is my heart, Ches. Please don't break it. "I trust you," she repeated.

She straightened her back, squared her shoulders, and placed her hands loosely on her lap.

Ches crooked his head, watching the transformation from panic to peace. He clicked his tongue and said, "Hyep, hyep." Then he led Lad and Grace on the path to the house.

At the porch, Ches directed her on how to dismount. With only the guidance from his hand, she'd done it, hitting the ground with both feet supremely proud of herself. She grinned up at him.

"I did it."

He returned her smile with a big one of his own. "Yep."

Grace patted Lad's neck then brought her arm up and

in as close to a hug she could muster between human and horse. "Thank you, Lad, for letting me ride you. You are so beautiful." Pat. Pat. Pat. "And strong to carry me on your back." Pat. Pat. Pat.

She ran her hand along his beautiful coat one last time.

"I'm going to take him back to the paddock. Go on inside, if you like. There's some towels in the laundry room on top of the dryer."

"Is that where he was when you called him?"

"Yes. He'll jump the fence if I whistle for him, which doesn't happen too often, does it, boy?" Ches walked toward the barn and the enclosed fence next to it. Grace watched him go and the horse following like a duckling behind his momma.

Grace entered the house, and heard rapid footsteps approaching her. Haley appeared, her fearful expression meeting Grace's. "Where's Pop?"

Sunni followed, her face guarded.

"He's fine. He went to put Lad away."

"Lad? What was he doing out?" Haley asked.

"I lost one of my shoes, so he let me ride back to the house."

The little girl's mouth fell open. "He let you ride Laddie? You're kidding."

"No."

"Pop hardly lets anybody ride Laddie. He must really like you."

"I think it was a matter of making sure I didn't step on anything sharp on the walk back."

Haley shook her head. "I wanna go outside to see Poppy." She shot toward the door.

"Hold on, Haley. Pop will be here in a few minutes. I'm sure he doesn't want to have to look for you if you happen to miss each other. Why don't you help me find a towel before I get the whole floor wet?"

Haley dutifully picked up a towel from the floor. "Here. You can use the one I used."

Sunni stepped into the room, took the towel Haley

offered, and replaced it with a folded one from the clothes basket resting on top of the dryer.

"Thanks, Sunni."

"When's Pop getting back? I think we ought to check on him." Haley had on dry clothes, but her hair was tangled and wet.

"Oh, my goodness. It looks like your hair needs to be combed."

The little girl reached her hands to her scalp. "No, it doesn't."

"Oh, dear me, yes."

"Don't touch it!" She wrapped her arms around her head.

Grace smiled and dried herself as best she could. "I certainly won't right now. I'm taking care of my own untidiness. I'm sure my hair has plenty of tangles, too, after the dip in the pond."

Haley craned her head, examining Grace. "Rats' nest," she declared.

"Excuse me?"

"Your hair. It's a rats' nest." A mischievous smile settled on Haley's face.

Well, that was a new one. Grace looked at Sunni who pursed her lips. "That's what Dad calls hair when it has a lot of tangles."

"Bring your brush to me, please," Grace said to Haley.

"No way, man."

"Why not?" Grace gave the little girl an innocent look. "Don't you want me to get the rats' nests out of my hair?"

"You're gonna brush my hair, ain't cha?"

"How am I going to do that unless you give me permission to?"

"You'll say, 'Sit still, Haley, or no ice cream!'"

Grace shook her head. "Sweet girl, I don't have authority over the ice cream in this house."

The door opened, and Ches entered, his shirt clinging to him, his boots making a squashing noise with each step he took. A look passed between him and Sunni. It was quick, but intense. The young woman stiffened.

"Pop!" Haley flung herself at him, and he reached down, caught her, and lifted her in his arms. She began to cry, her arms wrapping around him.

Picking up on Haley's distress, Jojo barked and loped to Ches, sitting at his feet.

"I was so scared, Pop, and then you were under the water."

"Shh, shh. I'm fine, Little Bit." He petted her back for a moment. "Shh. Shh. Everything is okay. I promise." He set her down on the floor and gave Jojo a perfunctory pat on his head before reaching for a towel from the dryer. "Let me get some dry clothes on now." He met Grace's gaze. "You okay?"

She nodded.

His gaze ran over her as if reassuring himself she was telling him the truth. He nodded. "All right then."

He'd watched Haley flail in the water before saving her and almost drowning himself. He'd taken the time to put Lad away before coming in the house. He was making sure everyone was taken care of before he himself took care of his own needs. This was probably why he'd had a heart attack a few weeks ago. Everyone else's health and wellbeing came first.

He walked into the kitchen, then beyond it. As if he were the grand marshal at a parade, everyone followed: Haley, Jojo, Sunni, then Grace herself.

At the stairs, the parade dispersed. Ches went up to the second story; everyone else lingered in the room. Only Jojo settled on a large pillow in the corner. Not wanting to get the furniture wet, Grace stood. She should go home, but it felt wrong to leave without saying goodbye to Ches. Still. She could call him later, even when she got home, to check on him. He must be in a turmoil of emotions.

"Wanna go to the ball pit?" Haley asked. Her troubled gaze jumped to where Ches was ascending the stairs then back to Grace.

"Sure."

She and Haley walked through the French doors to the room where they had played once before. Haley unzipped the opening all the way, obviously making room for Grace to enter. When they were settled inside, Haley looked around and picked up two purple balls. "Wanna play tic-tac-toe? We can throw 'em to make it harder."

"Okay."

"I'll be purple. What color do you want to be?"

"Doesn't matter. Red, I suppose."

They took turns throwing the balls at the criss-crossed target.

"Pop is okay, you know," Grace said.

Haley threw a ball, but it missed. She picked up another one and tossed it. It landed on the lower middle, leaving a spot open for Grace to win.

"Is that what's wrong?"

"Sunni yelled at me for falling in. But I didn't mean to. I was trying to get a lightning bug, and I got too close to the water. She told me to get off the pier, but I was being real careful."

Grace abandoned the game. "Well." She shrugged. "If you learn from this that next time you should do what Sunni says, then it's okay. It's what we call a life lesson."

The girl sighed. "Sunni started crying. She asked me why I did it, but I didn't mean to."

"I know, honey."

Chapter Ten

In dry clothes, Ches opened the door of his bedroom.

Little Bit could have died. If I hadn't been there, she would have. And if Grace hadn't been there, I would have died. Leaving my girls with no one to take care of them. No one.

He walked down the stairs. Movement caught his eye. Sunni. She stood near the bottom of the railing, her stiff posture demonstrative of her battle-ready state.

He wasn't in the mood—wasn't up for another screaming match.

"So, are you going to send Haley off like you did Cinnamon?"

"You know better than that." Ches stepped down the last stair and crossed to the kitchen. Where was Grace? Had she left already?

Sunni followed him. "Of course not. You wouldn't want anything to happen to your precious Little Bit. Maybe you can actually do things right with her. Unlike how you and Mom threw me back and forth to each other until you got the short straw and had to keep me."

Ches turned to face her. Keep calm. No matter what, don't let her get to you. She's upset. She knows tonight could have ended bad. Really bad.

Patiently, he spoke. "We didn't throw you back and forth. I wanted to keep you. Your mother gave me no choice until she sent you back."

"That's not how she tells it."

"I can't help what she says."

"You can help that you are ready to throw me back now."

"You're not a ball, Sunni. You're a grown woman. If you want to go to Illinois to live with your mother, then go."

Sunni's nostrils flared. "Don't do that. I hate it when

you do that."

Ches leaned back against the counter—nearly the same spot he had when he'd had that searing pain in his chest that had radiated down his arm.

"Do what?"

"Act like you're doing me some great big favor by giving me permission to go."

He'd gotten to where he couldn't breathe, like he had a pallet of hay sitting on his chest.

"What do you want me to do? Demand you stay here? Forbid you to ever leave Wren's Fork?"

"You sold Cinnamon so I wouldn't have a reason to stay here."

Sunni's horse again. "Cinnamon is gone. There's no reason to bring him up."

"Why won't you tell me who you sold him to, Dad? You're just mean. Horrible and mean."

He'd tried to ignore the pain and the heavy weight on his chest as he and Sunni had argued, but it had gotten harder and harder. He remembered reaching up and rubbing his pectoral muscle, then wiping the sweat pouring off his forehead.

"It's done. I can't take it back, and you can't go see him."

"You can take it back. You can get him back. You just don't want to."

Now, there was no pain. No weight. He took a deep breath in and out. He actually felt pretty darn good physically.

Even though he'd swallowed a pint or two of pond water. The heart medicine must be working.

He shook his head. "He's gone, Sunni. You need to put him out of your mind and move on."

"Move on with my life. Leave here. That's what you mean. You don't want me here. If you did, you wouldn't have sold him. How much did you sell him for, huh? What did you do with the money?"

"Do you want the money? I'll put it in your account

Monday."

"I don't want the money. I want my horse."

"Well, that's not going to happen. Not ever."

"Cinnamon was my horse. Mine! You had no right. None." She took a shuddering breath. And the despondent light of her eyes nearly undid him. "How could you sell him and take him away without letting me say goodbye? I hate you for that, and I'll never forgive you."

It sounded like a great exit line. Obviously, Sunni thought so, too. She stalked out of the kitchen, through the pantry and slammed the door leading to the garage. The grinding noise of the outer door opening in unison with her car starting told him she was not only leaving the house, but the farm.

One day she'd leave and not come back. He knew it—knew she wanted to, but hadn't worked up enough courage or enough anger toward him to do it. Ches wished she'd either make peace with staying here or go ahead and go. These fights drained him, made him question if he'd done the right thing about Cinnamon.

He couldn't tell Sunni what really happened. The truth would be much harder on her, and though she was an adult, Ches had decided he wanted to shield her from more pain.

It was better this way.

He'd be the bad guy, and she would eventually get over losing Cinnamon and forgive him.

He hoped.

He peeked out the window and saw Sunni's retreating vehicle. Next to the drive was Grace's car where she'd parked it earlier. Good. She was still here—had probably heard most, if not all, of the argument between him and Sunni. Ches recalled the words they had exchanged. Yes, he had stayed calm, and he hadn't been cruel. Unless you consider selling Sunni's horse without her knowledge cruel.

Had they gone back outside? He didn't think so. He walked through the living room and saw the French door ajar. Going through it, he walked into the sunroom and saw the ball pit zipper gaping open.

Aha.

He stepped through and what he saw caused his poor heart to turn in his chest.

Haley sat on a small stool in front of Grace who brushed her hair.

"Hi, Pop," Haley said.

Ches swallowed once, twice, before he could speak. He lowered himself amidst the many balls.

"Little Bit. Miss Grace."

"Miss Grace is brushing my hair, and she's being real gentle. It hardly hurts."

"Is that so?"

Grace shot him a conspiratorial wink, and, my, my, his heart hitched. So, this is what the medicine does for him: keeps his heart fine in stressful arguments, but in tender moments, turns his heart to mush. He'd have to ask the doctor about this. Could crushing on a woman give him another heart attack?

The thought made him smile.

"She says there's this spray you buy at the store. It's magic. You put it on your hair and the rats just leave."

"Hmm."

"Since she didn't have any, she had to use olive oil. She keeps a little bottle of it in her purse."

"She does?"

"Tell him, Miss Grace, all the stuff you use olive oil for."

She smiled. "Mainly, for anointing, but in a pinch it's good for dry skin and tangled hair."

"She don't like to call tangled up hair rats and rats' nests, Pop. She says it's...." Haley shifted her head slightly. Ches noticed Grace moved her hand so she wouldn't pull the child's hair. "What's that word again?"

"Uncouth." Grace waited, perhaps to see if Haley would move her head again. When she didn't, the woman held a lock of hair and dabbed a bit of oil on it. She combed it then without any resistance.

"You ever heard that word, Pop? Uncouth."

She was beautiful. He wanted to set Little Bit away from her and take her in his arms, kiss her, tell her how much she already meant to him, how it scared him to think such things.

"A time or two maybe."

"Miss Grace said if I let her brush my hair, she'd let me brush hers."

"I don't know. It's getting late, and somebody needs to be getting a bath and to bed."

"That mean you and Sunni are done with your fight? Whew, I could hear every word. And if there's going to be more yelling, I ain't gonna be able to sleep."

Grace didn't meet his eyes over Haley's head. What had she thought of what she'd heard?

"It wasn't a fight. Just a disagreement."

"I wish you hadn't sold Cinnamon. I thought you liked horses." The accusatory tone in the four-year-old's voice wasn't lost on him.

"I do like horses."

"Then why'd you get rid of him?"

Oh, Lord. What answer could he give to Little Bit that would satisfy her? He hadn't come up with anything yet that had smoothed things over with Sunni.

"There," Grace said. "I think those are most of the tangles. Want to brush my hair for a few minutes, then you can get your bath."

"Okay." Haley hopped up, and Grace scooted forward, meeting Ches' gaze as she did so. Her knowing glance told him she'd deliberately distracted Haley. With the brush in her hand, Haley moved it through Grace's hair. "Oh. Here's a rat...umm...tangle, I mean. Better give me the olive oil."

Surprised, Ches watched Grace hand her the small bottle. "Remember just a little dab."

He suppressed a chuckle. Yeah, this was going to end well.

"Ooops." Haley's face registered shock then despair. "Oh, no! I spilled it."

"That's all right, sweetie. Just brush it out. Here, give me the bottle, and I'll hold it."

"I'll get something to get it up." Ches moved toward the opening, regretting that he had to leave the small space to get a towel.

"Ches," Grace said.

He stopped and looked back at her.

"It's okay. I think most of it is in my hair. It's fine." She smiled, her kind eyes inviting him to be calm, to be at peace. It's good. It was all good.

"Miss Grace, would you give me my bath tonight?"

"If it's all right with Pop, yes, though I have to tell you, I've never given a little girl a bath before."

"You was a little girl once. Didn't you bathe yourself?"

"Well, yes, but that was a long time ago."

"She probably needs to get home and get out of her wet clothes," Ches said attempting to give Grace a gracious excuse to leave.

"Oh, Pop, can't you just let her wear your pants again?"

Ches blew a breath out. Oh, boy. "Well, she...umm...."

"I think I could make it work with sweat pants and a shirt."

She could make it work with sweat pants and a shirt. Really?

Without waiting for a reply, she rose and exited the tent with Haley behind her. Ches headed to the pantry once again. He found a pair of his basketball shorts and one of his T-shirts in a basket of clean clothes waiting to be folded.

"Sugar, will shorts be all right?" He called to her from the pantry.

"Yes," she called back.

"Want to just take a bath down here, Little Bit?" he asked as he also found a pair of Little Bit's pajamas and underwear. He held up the tiny undergarment wondering if he should ask Grace if she needed some too. But he couldn't think of a diplomatic way to ask.

She said she could make pants and shirt work. That's *all* he needed to know.

They appeared with Little Bit's smile a mile wide. She loved the big tub, but rarely got to bathe in it, as by this time of night, he had already shepherded her upstairs.

With Grace taking care of bath time, Ches used the time to do a load of towels and tackle the mountain of clean clothes perpetually resting on the dryer. He listened to the conversation between Grace and Haley amidst to water sounds as he folded and in between trips upstairs to put away the clothes.

She was so good with Haley, so patient and kind. He loved that about her. Loved that she was so sweet to the little girl when she didn't have to be.

How come Grace wasn't married with children of her own?

When he'd asked her the night they met, she said no one had ever asked to marry her. Ches found that hard to believe. How come men weren't beating down her door to date her? It couldn't just be because of her height. Was it because of her faith? Had she decided to only marry someone who shared her belief in God? If so, why was she still giving him the time of day? He'd been clear that he didn't believe in a god who killed babies and mommies of 12 year old boys, like his mom.

But Grace experienced those awful moments with families at the hospital, and her faith was rock solid. What had she said?

The god you don't believe in is the one who always answers prayers the way we want him to. I don't believe in that god either.

She didn't believe in that god either. The God she believes in was the one who sat with her atop of Laddie. Ches had watched with awe the transformation from skittish amateur to calm and confident rider when he invoked the name of her God. Presence, she said. Presence was important to her. That she was never alone with the

Lord, her God. The knowledge had chased away her fear and allowed her to sit tall and proud on Lad.

Grace didn't realize it, but Ches didn't let just anyone ride his horse. She was the only female other than Sunni and Haley. The moment had been like giving her a promise ring, a practice in high school of the boys, including himself, who had serious girlfriends. The promise ring was a pre-cursor to the engagement ring. He'd given one to Vanessa, then an engagement ring, then a wedding ring. But Vanessa had never ridden his horse.

Not even once.

"Why don't you take a bath with me?" Ches heard Little Bit ask Grace from the other side of the mostly shut door.

"No, dear."

"How come? The tub's plenty big enough. I love this tub because it's like swimming in a pool."

"Can you swim, Haley?"

"Well, I think I can. I mean, I do well in here. But any time I swim in a big pool, I've got my floaties on. I didn't have my floaties tonight, and I was surprised when I fell in."

"Perhaps you and I can go to the pool some time, and I can teach you how to swim. That way, if you ever fall in again, you'll know what to do."

"You can get in now and show me what to do."

Grace chuckled. "We'll do it another time in a pool. It will be much easier to show you what to do then."

"Can Jojo get in the tub with me?"

"Sweetheart, bathing is really an individual event. It's something most of us do by ourselves."

"I've bathed with Jojo before."

Ches opened his mouth to defend the one time *he knew of* that Haley and Jojo had ended up in the tub together, but Grace's laughter stopped him.

"Well, tonight, let's just let it be you in the tub, all right?" she said.

After her bath, Haley insisted on Grace tucking her in

as well. Ches hung back and watched the interaction between woman and child, his heart strings tugging him ever closer to Grace and the kind affection she offered to his niece who was like a daughter to him.

"Will you pray that prayer again, the one you said when we went to the wedding? I've tried to remember it, but I can't."

Ches couldn't see Grace's face since her back was to him.

"I tell you what I'll do. I'll write it down and give it to Pop. Then you'll always have it. All right?"

"Okay."

"For now, I'll say it a little at a time, and you can repeat it. Close your eyes."

"Why do we close our eyes to pray?" Haley asked.

Grace shrugged. "I honestly don't know. It's just how I was taught to pray."

"Can I keep my eyes open?"

"I suppose so. Do you want me to keep my eyes open, too?"

"Yes."

Grace spoke the prayer phrase by phrase and guided Haley through it by repetition. The girl stumbled a few times, and Grace patiently corrected her. When they arrived at the amen, Haley reached forward and hugged Grace. She whispered something to her, but Ches didn't catch it.

"Aw," Grace intoned. "I love you, too, Haley." She patted her back. "I am so glad God brought you into my life."

Haley lay back down. "Why'd He do it?"

"What?"

"Why did God brought me into your life?"

"Oh, lots of reasons, probably."

"Maybe to teach me to swim."

"Perhaps."

"And for someone to go to the wedding with."

"Yes."

"And to love me."

"Yes, that too."

"And to love Pop."

Grace didn't reply.

"And Sunni. She needs a lot of love."

"We all do. Sweet dreams, little one." Grace stood, bent down, and kissed Haley's forehead.

"Sweet dreams, big one," Haley said.

Ches snickered, and heard Grace echo his sentiment. Relieved she didn't take offense at Little Bit's comment or his answering chuckle, his opinion of the woman rose even higher, if that were possible.

Haley turned to her side and closed her eyes, not waiting for Ches to bid her good night. Grace moved aside and glanced back at him. He walked to Haley's bedside, cupped her small shoulder, and kissed her baby-soft cheek.

"Love you," he murmured into her hair.

"Love you, too, Pop," she whispered without opening her eyes.

He watched her for a moment. How he loved this child. His thoughts turned to Sunni when she had been Haley's age, when he had tucked her in and kissed her goodnight. Would Haley, at nineteen, be the angry, resentful woman that Sunni was now?

What could he do to make things right between him and Sunni? He couldn't tell her the truth; it would devastate her. And even before the business with Cinnamon had happened, he and Sunni hadn't been okay. She'd withdrawn from him, and he'd known she'd wanted to leave. After all, she had enough of her mother in her not to live on a farm her whole life tending to corn and cows. He loved her enough to let her go.

Grace stood in the corner of the room, giving Ches space to be Pop to Haley. Ches was once again struck by the height of the woman. He stood apart from her, but close enough that his frame shadowed her from the soft lamp glowing on Haley's chest of drawers.

"Can you stay a little longer?"

Her lips curved into a small smile, as if he'd guessed a

secret she'd been keeping, one she'd been hoping to share with him.

He inclined his head, inviting her to proceed him out of the room. He followed her down the stairs noticing she'd put her hair in a ponytail, probably to help with the spilled olive oil. Her hair was the color of the corn silk before harvest. Ches raised his hand to touch it to determine if her hair was as soft, but resisted. He doubted she'd swoon knowing he was comparing her hair to a corn plant. And his thoughts were too jumbled to come up with another excuse to touch her.

"Would it be all right if Haley spent part of tomorrow with me? I can feed her lunch and have her back to you by two."

"I suppose. It'd actually help me out a bit, as I've got some cows calving, and I'm not sure if Sunni will be around tomorrow morning. If she isn't, I'll have to take Little Bit out with me, which is fine, I do that sometimes, but it's a whole lot easier if I'm by myself."

"Great. What time do you need to leave in the morning?"

"Tell you what, why don't we meet halfway between here and Carlton? That way you don't have to drive all the way here," Ches said.

"Eight is fine, and I can keep her longer if you need me to."

"Can I let you know tomorrow?"

"Of course." She shifted from one foot to the other. Ches wondered if she were nervous. What should they do now? He hadn't entertained a woman in his house in so long, he'd forgotten how.

"Want to sit on the porch?" he asked as he picked up the baby monitor he used when Haley was in her room and he wasn't close enough to hear her if she needed him.

They settled on the porch swing about the same distance apart they'd been before he'd heard Sunni calling for him.

The chorus of crickets filled the night air, and the light

from the yard pole didn't diminish the sparks of the lightning bugs dotting the landscape.

"Ches?" she said finally. "Do you want to talk about it?"

He placed his arm across the back of the swing, his fingers encountering her hair. He smiled. Success. Unwilling to bring up the church subject again, he played dumb. "Which *it* do you mean? I've had several of them tonight."

"Whichever *it* you want."

Ches moved a little closer to her. "Guess you're wondering what's going on with me and Sunni."

"You sold her horse, and she's upset about it."

"I'm horrible and mean."

"I'm sure you did what was best for everyone involved, including Cinnamon. One day, after some time has passed, Sunni may be able to understand that."

A lump formed in Ches' throat. Grace didn't know the whole story, but she was right. He had done what was best for Cinnamon. It was one of the hardest things he'd ever done in his life, but he'd done it.

"Where did she go?"

"I don't know. I suppose she drives around for a while or to a friend's house."

"Do you ever worry she won't come back?"

"One day she won't. She's a grown woman now. That day is coming soon."

"Because she wants to live with her mother?"

"Because she's her mother's daughter."

"Wouldn't you worry about her?"

Ches didn't answer for a moment. "She's an adult. If she leaves, she leaves. I can't stop her."

"What if she leaves and doesn't stay gone, would you let her come back and live with you and Haley again?"

"Of course. She's always welcome here. This is her home."

"Have you ever told her?"

Ches made a sound of dismissal. "She knows."

"Are you sure? Have you ever said those words to her, that she's always welcome here, that this is her home?"

He moved uncomfortably. "I probably have."

"Ches." Now it was Grace's turn to scoot closer to him, not that he could really appreciate it since she was putting him on the hot seat.

"All right," he admitted. "I don't recall saying those exact words. But she knows."

"Perhaps you can make sure she knows by saying them to her."

Ches studied Grace's profile, in awe of the wisdom and graciousness of this woman. "Would you really marry me just to make sure my girls were taken care of?"

She looked at him, then, amusement blanketing her features. "Changing the subject, huh?"

"Yep."

"I'd consider marrying you if you were dying and there was no one else to take care of them."

"Only if I were dying, huh?"

"But you're not dying."

"I could have died tonight." The truth of the statement should have scared him, but it didn't. As long as Grace was around, it seemed he was safe.

"As long as you're taking care of yourself, you'll live to be old."

"I've been told I'm a good catch." He moved another couple of inches closer. He could feel the warmth of her body near him, catch the sweet scent of her over the lilac bush next to the porch.

Grace chuckled. "You're a great catch, I'm sure, but I'm not—" Grace gasped.

"You're not what?"

Grace didn't speak for a moment.

"What's wrong?"

She shook her head. She breathed in and out, almost as if she were meditating. Finally, she said, "Ches, can I ask you a question?"

"I suppose." She didn't consider him marriage

material, did she? Why was that? Because he worked a ranch? Because of his heart condition? What?

"Did your mother name you?"

"Yep."

"What's the significance of your name, Chesapeake?"

"It was her maiden name. Lillith Cecille Chesapeake Larson."

Grace moved her body to face him. "Do you realize you have just lived through events that killed both of your parents? You survived a heart attack that killed your dad, and you survived a near drowning, the thing that killed your mom."

Ches blinked attempting to absorb her words. He had survived, hadn't he?

"So, see? You don't need me to marry you and take care of your girls. You're going to be around a long time."

Ches closed the distance between them and settled his arm around her shoulders. "Would it be so awful to be married to me for 40 or 50 years, sugar? You act like you ain't interested in the job, and that hurts my feelings a little."

She was close, so close all he'd have to do was move his face a few inches to kiss her. "I'm sorry. I don't mean to hurt your feelings. Why don't you stop talking and kiss me for a few minutes before I have to go?"

Ches grinned. He didn't even mind that Miss Grace was playing hard to get and being bossy at the same time. He dipped his head, and whispered. "Much obliged."

Chapter Eleven

Come with me and I will make you fishers of men.

That's the phrase which had marched across Grace's brain when Ches had said he was a good catch.

Grace had responded, *You're a great catch, I'm sure, but I'm not fishing.*

Well, that's what she had started to say.

She got as far as, *You're a great catch, I'm sure, but I'm not....*

Then Jesus had interrupted her.

Come with me, and I will make you fishers of men.

"Lord," Grace said aloud in the darkened car on her drive home. "I know when you said that, you were not talking about dating. You were talking to Peter about evangelism. Ches was teasing me about getting married. But I shouldn't get serious about a man who doesn't even believe in You."

Grace liked Ches. Maybe she was even falling in love with him. But she would not consider marrying him unless he was committed to the Lord God. That's just all there was to it.

"What are you doing, Lord? Is this You telling me it's okay to love him, or is this my heart playing tricks on me?"

The only answer Grace heard was the air conditioner humming in the interior of the car and the sound of the tires along the highway.

Grace sighed.

Should she have called Ches on his teasing? Should she have told him why marriage wasn't on the table? This was silly. Of course, he wasn't serious. They had known each other only a few weeks. He wouldn't propose marriage to someone after such a short period of time.

He was teasing her.

Of course he was.

But even if he wasn't, she would not marry a man who didn't believe in God.

"Lord, if you're asking me to catch Chesapeake Larson, I'll catch him for You. When You have him hook, line, and sinker, only then will I get out my fishing pole. All right?"

A sign would be good though. Just to be sure I understand what you want.

****

Ches and Grace had agreed to meet at a roadside park in Oakara so Haley could spend the day with Grace. When Grace maneuvered her car into a parking space, Ches' truck was already there, and he and Haley were standing at a picnic table.

Haley wore a pink crinoline dress and her cowboy boots with matching pink bow in her hair. Ches, obviously dressed for work, had in faded denim jeans and a T-shirt. His back was to the road, watching Haley as she marched across the bench. He had his ball cap on, and when he turned toward Grace's car, he reached up and adjusted the bill, lifting it, perhaps to see her better.

Haley jumped down and ran toward her car, arriving before Grace had opened the door.

"Hi," she shouted.

"Good morning," Grace returned. "You look very pretty today."

Haley smiled. Grabbing her skirt on either side, she spread it out and rocked back on her heels. She looked down at herself. "I sure do, don't I?"

Grace laughed and looked at Ches to see his reaction. His eyes met hers. Though he smiled, there was a seriousness in his gaze.

What was wrong?

"Did Sunni get back okay?"

He nodded.

"Still not speaking to you?"

He shrugged. "She got in late, and is still asleep. Thank you for doing this. Little Bit told me you all were going to church."

"Yes, we are," Haley said coming up beside them and taking Grace's hand. "We'll see you later, Pop."

"Now wait just a minute." He strode to his truck and retrieved a small flowery duffel bag and Haley's carseat. Setting the seat on the ground and handing the tote to Grace, he said, "A change of clothes for later, and I'll put her carseat in for you." He knelt before Haley. "How about a hug and a kiss for your old Pop?"

Haley jumped into his arms and he embraced her. "Love you." He leaned away from her. "Best behavior, please ma'am."

"Of course, Pop. Who do ya think you're talking to?"

Watching the love and tenderness between the two caused a lump to form in Grace's throat. She stepped back, as if that would remove the intensity of her feelings for him.

Yes, him. Chesapeake Larson.

Ches reached forward and kissed the tip of her nose. "I'm talking to my Little Bit, that's who. Behave yourself, or Miss Grace has my permission to put you in a corner." He stood with that warning.

Haley placed her hands on her hips and marched over to Grace's car. "Now, we both know no one's getting put in the corner today."

Ches picked up the carseat and moved to the car. "I hope not, young lady." He opened the back door of Grace's Ford Focus and placed the seat in the middle, belting it in. Backing out of the car, he motioned for Haley to climb in. "Sugar," he said to Grace. "Why don't you get on the other side, so I can show you how to buckle her in."

Ches demonstrated the mechanics of the seat, and when the child was securely inside, both adults rose. Their gazes met over the hood of the car.

"I'll take good care of her, as if she were my own," Grace said.

One side of his mouth turned up, as if he wouldn't quite commit to the smile. "I know."

She walked around the car and stood in front of him. "Is it something you want to tell me now, or shall we talk about it later?"

The smile won. "Sugar, I don't quite know what to make of you. I've never known anyone who can feel the undercurrents of my psyche like you can."

Grace stepped closer and took his hand. His fingers closed around hers. "It's called empathy. I've been told I'm very good at it."

"Little Bit has never been to church."

Ah. "I'm sorry. I should have asked you if it was okay. She asked if she could come. I didn't think you'd mind since you allow me to pray with her."

"I...." Ches sighed. "I wish I could see what you see at the hospital, know what you know about how people suffer and die and still be okay with it. I wish I had that kind of faith."

"I've read it just takes a tiny-sized mustard seed to blossom in a flourishing tree where birds can perch and rest. Faith is like that. It has to grow."

Ches' beautiful eyes watched her, steadily. His grasp tightened. "I want to kiss you. Really want to."

"All right."

He snorted in humor and shook his head in irony. "All right. As if it will all be all right."

Grace closed the distance between them and put her arms around him. "And all shall be well, and all shall be well, and in all manner of things, it shall be well."

"Who said that?"

"Me and Julian of Norwich." Rising on tip-toes, she tilted her face. Ches accepted her invitation, giving her a gentle kiss.

"Hey! Hey! Let's get this show on the road, Miss Grace," Haley yelled from the car.

With chuckles, they separated with a promise to talk in the afternoon if Ches couldn't get away to meet them at their designated meeting place.

Grace enjoyed the novelty of taking a child to church,

felt pride as the people of church complimented Haley as she preened under the praise, and a bit of trepidation when she left her in the children's Sunday school class. Haley was as good as gold, sitting quietly in worship coloring the pages provided to children to occupy them if they needed an activity. After church, Grace made lunch at her house— sandwiches and apple slices.

"Do you always eat tuna fish sandwiches for lunch?" Haley asked as they sat at her kitchen table.

"Most Sundays I do."

"Don't you get lonely eating here by yourself?"

"Not too much. And if I need company, I can invite someone from church to eat with me."

"Or me, Pop, and Sunni."

"Sure."

"Pop works most Sundays. He says cows don't care what day it is."

"They get hungry no matter what day it is," Grace confirmed.

"And they try to get out no matter what day it is. Pop's always running fences cause if cows get out and get hit, it's his fault. Not the cow's. Cows are dumb, for the most part."

"Really?"

"Yeah. I like your tuna fish. Pop puts celery in his sandwich, and it crunches. I only like celery and tuna fish if it's boat people."

"What?"

Haley blinked at her. "Don't you know what boat people are?"

Grace shook her head.

"Well, you cut a celery like it's a boat, and you spread tuna fish and mayonnaise on it, then you stick pecan halves on it, like they're people in the boat. Pop brings 'em for me when we go fishing, but he makes a sandwich for himself cause he says it's less messy when he's holding a fishing pole."

"Huh. Well, I've never eaten boat people before."

"It's good. You gotta try it some time."

"Yes, I will."

Ches had texted to say he couldn't get away by two, and if she wanted to wait until later, he could drove over to Carlton and pick up Haley. Grace returned that she'd drive Haley home whenever it was convenient for him to be done with work, and she and the little girl went to see a movie matinee. Nearing six, Grace brought the child home. Sunni sat at a desk in the corner at a computer. She turned as they entered the house.

"Hi," she said. "Where've you been?"

"I spent the day with Miss Grace. We went to a movie and everything."

Sunni studied first Haley then Grace.

"You could come along next time, if you like," Grace said.

"I've got a big paper due, and the Internet keeps kicking off. I hate living in the country."

"I live in the city, and mine does that sometimes, usually when there's a rain storm."

"Guess it stinks everywhere." She turned back to the computer and began typing.

The door opened, and Jojo loped inside followed by Ches—his clothes covered in dirt and grime. His hair, wet from perspiration, curled above his ears, testifying he'd worn a hat most of the day. He smiled, and his teeth gleamed from his work-smudged skin. "I thought I heard your car, Sugar."

"Pop!" Haley launched herself in his arms.

"Hey, Little Bit, how was it, spending all day with Miss Grace?"

"It was great." She began a monologue of all the things they had done that day as Ches held her, walking into the kitchen while she chattered.

Grace sat on the couch, and to her surprise, Sunni claimed the recliner closest to her. The act felt like a gift to Grace, and she wanted to acknowledge it.

"You know," she said. "I have a friend at the library in

town. She says their Internet is very reliable, and they have study rooms you can reserve for two hours at a time."

Sunni rolled her eyes. "In Carlton? That's almost an hour away."

Grace shrugged. "45 Minutes, and the library is actually a little closer than that, on Hwy 5 as you come into town."

"Oh." She glanced at the doorway to the kitchen where Haley's voice still carried. "So, I guess Dad asked you to keep Haley."

"No. She asked to go to church with me today."

Sunni's eyebrows rose. "Really? Huh. I guess you being a chaplain, it's required."

Grace smiled. "No, but I like going."

"Dad doesn't trust me with Haley anymore."

"Did he tell you that?"

"He didn't have to. I know he won't. I almost let her drown, and then he almost...." She took a shuttering breath.

Grace leaned forward. "Sunni, you called out for your dad when Haley was in danger, and you needed help. Loud and clear. He heard you, and he came. So did I. Everyone is okay because you were paying attention, and you called for your dad. You were the reason Haley is okay."

"I should have gone after her myself."

"And if you had, things could have turned out really bad. I knew what to do because I've been trained as lifeguard. I think it was providential for me to have been here."

"You mean, like, you were supposed to be here?"

Grace smiled. "Yes."

Sunni shook her head. "Where was providence when Dad sold Cinnamon?"

"I know it hurts that he did that, but what can you do about it now?"

"Nothing. Unless I can find out who he sold him to. He won't tell me." Her gaze dropped, then she pierced Grace with her attention. "He'd tell you, Grace, if you asked him."

"Oh, honey—"

Sunni leaned forward, tears sparkling in her eyes. "Please? I know I probably can't get him back. Dad thinks I'm not responsible enough to keep a horse."

"Why would he think that?"

"Because I left the gate open a few times. It's kind of a pain to lock, so sometimes I just shut it, and it doesn't always catch. But to sell my horse for that." She shook her head. "It's like he doesn't even care about my feelings, what's important to me, that it was a mistake."

Grace sighed. "Listen, your dad seems to be a reasonable person. I don't think he would sell Cinnamon unless he had a really good reason to. Have you tried talking to him, calmly, about it?"

"It's… umm…hard to be calm about it."

Grace reached for the young woman's hands and cradled them in her own. "I can tell you're trying. That's good. That's a good thing. If you can be calm like this with him, I think it would help, okay?" She squeezed her hands for emphasis.

Sunni nodded. "If I don't get better luck here with the Internet, I might come over to the library."

"You've already got my cell number, but I'll text you my address, too. If you are up that way, you can stop by the house."

Sunni smiled. It was the first genuine smile Grace had seen on her face.

Haley ran in the room then. "Miss Grace, guess what!" The little girl jumped up and down in her excitement. Ches strolled in the room carrying a stadium cup. He paused, waiting on Haley to speak. "Pop said we could go fishing, and he'd fix you some boat people."

Go fishing?

Grace looked from Haley to Ches and back again. She shook her head, at a loss as to how to respond. "I… don't…." Her throat closed with emotion.

Come with me, and I will make you fishers of men.

"If you don't have a fishing pole, we could loan you

one, right, Pop?"

"Yep."

"And we could eat boat people, and Sunni, you'd come, too, wouldn't you?" Haley said. "We'd have so much fun."

"Yes." Sunni hesitated. "It would be fun. We haven't gone fishing in a long time."

"What do you say, Sugar? Want to go fishing?" Ches asked.

Grace swallowed. Here was a sign if there ever was one. No subtlety here, Lord. Nope. This sign was like a ton of bricks avalanching down around Grace in the form of a very tall handsome man and his two sweet girls. A bubble of humor escaped Grace's mouth in the form of a chortle. Then another. Soon, Grace was bent over laughing.

"I don't get it. What's so funny about fishing?" Sunni asked.

"Probably eating boat people," Haley decided.

Ches placed his hand on the stair rail. "I'm going to take a shower. If she lets you in on the joke before I get back, be sure to tell me. I hate to miss out on something so amusing."

****

Grace awoke with a start. At first, she thought it was the pager alerting her she had an emergency at the hospital, but then she remembered she wasn't on call. Sitting up, she picked up her cell phone and looked at it. The text icon showed she had four messages. Touching the screen to open them, she noted they were all from Sunni.

Fight w/ Dad. RUhome. RUthere. Need2Talk.

The doorbell pealed twice, and Grace realized that was the sound she'd heard. Throwing back the covers, she texted Sunni.

Are you at my front door?

Yes came the reply.

It was almost two in the morning. What had happened?

Turning on lights as she made her way through the

house, Grace unlocked the door. There stood Sunni, all in black including the smeared make-up around her eyes. She stared at Grace with an expression of anger.

Grace stepped back, opening the door wider. "Come in, Sweetheart."

The young woman's shoulders drooped, as if relieved. She entered, and Grace closed the door, leading her into the sitting room.

"Are you thirsty?"

Sunni shook her head.

"Sit down."

Obediently, she did. Grace perched on the cushion next to her. "Are you okay?"

Sunni shrugged.

What? Did Grace need to leave the room and text the young woman before she'd tell her what was going on?

"Do you want to talk about it, Sunni?" she asked.

"I don't know."

Grace studied the young woman before her. Exhaustion radiated from her like heat waves on summer pavement.

"Tell you what. Why don't you go to the bathroom, wash your face and get cleaned up a little? I'll make up the guest bedroom and you can get some sleep, then we'll talk about it in the morning. Okay?"

"I don't know if I can sleep," Sunni said in a small voice.

"Well, try, and if you can't, come get me."

"Don't tell Dad I'm here."

"Please don't ask me to keep secrets from him. He's your father, and he loves you."

Sunni shook her head. "No, he doesn't, and I don't want him to know where I am."

"If you didn't want him to know where you were, then why would you come here?"

A tear trailed down Sunni's cheek. "I thought you would understand."

"I want to understand. I do, but if you don't go home,

Ches is going to worry."

"He isn't going to worry. He doesn't love me. He just tolerates me."

"Of course, he loves you. You're his daughter."

You've seen how he treats me compared to how he treats Haley."

"Haley's a child."

"Yeah, and obviously his favorite."

"You're nineteen, Sunni. An adult now. Maybe your dad is trying to treat you like an adult."

Sunni shook his head. "No. I don't believe that. If he were treating me like an adult, he wouldn't have sold my horse. He wouldn't have made such a big decision without at least asking me first."

Grace sat back. She wished she had an answer for why Ches did what he did. When she herself had given him the chance to talk about it, he had simply stated Sunni thought he was horrible and that had been it. Should Grace ask him about the horse and what had led him to sell? It really wasn't her business though.

Was it?

She and Ches were building something—whether friendship or more, Grace wasn't sure. She did believe God had given her a message concerning building that something. Grace was in love with him. Yes, she could admit that now. But how did he feel about her?

And would her getting involved with this disagreement between him and his daughter be a game changer for him?

Grace sighed. She had only dated a few men—only one seriously—and he hadn't had a daughter for Grace to have to figure out how to maneuver a relationship with.

What should she do?

When Grace didn't speak, Sunni continued. "You told me to be calm and talk to him. Ask him." Her appealing gaze tore at Grace. "Why won't he just tell me? I swore I wouldn't do anything dumb. I begged him, Grace, and he still wouldn't tell me."

Grace patted the young woman's hand. "I know he has

his reasons. You have to trust him that he's doing the right thing."

"But he's not. He hasn't. Not any of it. I just.... I can't live like this—knowing what he did. He knew how much I loved Cinnamon, and he didn't care. He still doesn't care."

This wasn't getting them anywhere. Grace stood. "Come on, honey. You're tired. Get some sleep, and tomorrow we'll sort it out, okay?"

Grace showed Sunni to the bathroom, then stepped to the closet at the end of the hallway and removed fresh linens. By the time Sunni entered the bedroom, Grace had made up the bed. She bid the young woman good night and went back to bed. It seemed only a minute passed when her alarm awoke her.

As was her custom, she took a cup of coffee, her Bible, and her journal out to the front porch. Instead of praying in her mind during her devotion time, she wrote her thoughts, joys, struggles, and prayers in her journal. Sometimes, the answers to her questions would pour out through the ink on the lined paper. Other times, a peace would fill her as she read over her recently written words, and Grace would close her journal with a contented sigh.

As she flipped through the pages of recent weeks, she noticed how often Ches' name appeared in her handwriting. He was a good man. If only he weren't so angry at God for the deaths of his parents.

Grace knew death was part of life. Pain was part of life, and it didn't lessen God's love for us when we suffered through loss or pain. Grace had found it was often in the most griping moments that God's peace sustained her when nothing else could. Is there something else she could be doing to demonstrate that for Ches, Sunni, and Haley?

No answer came except for the phrase that had parked itself in her brain.

Come with me, and I will make you fishers of men.

Grace smiled at the Larson family invitation to go fishing. Oh, my, if they had only known how wonderfully eerie their offer to include her in a fishing trip was in her own spiritual discernment.

It seemed too much of a coincidence. It seemed God was saying *Go get him, girl.*

If only it were that easy. But it wasn't just Ches' shaky faith Grace was faced with, but now how to handle her involvement in the volatile relationship between him and Sunni.

Grace showered and dressed, getting ready for her day at the hospital.

What should she do about her guest?

Chapter Twelve

Grace knocked at the other bedroom. "Sunni?"

Hearing a summons, Grace opened the door and stood at the threshold. From the light of the hallway, Grace saw Sunni in bed. She sat up in bed, wiping her eyes.

"I'm sorry to wake you so early," Grace said. "But I have to go to work at the hospital. Help yourself to food in the kitchen, and if you leave the house and want to come back later, I keep a spare key inside the little basket on the kitchen shelf next to the back door. Do you need anything before I go?"

"No ma'am."

Grace smiled at the reply. It was the first time the young woman demonstrated her knowledge of polite Southern etiquette.

And it only took a missing horse and a two am wake up call for Grace to hear it.

"You won't tell Daddy where I am, will you?"

Grace moved into the room and sat on the edge of the bed. Sunni's cautious gaze stayed on her.

What could she say that would open up the communication between father and daughter instead of shutting it down between her and said daughter?

"I won't tell him you're here because I know you are going to be an adult about this. Call or text him and tell him you need some time away, but you're all right."

Sunni didn't answer.

Grace waited a good ten seconds hoping Sunni would agree, but the young woman stayed silent. Standing up, Grace walked out of the room. "I'll be home by five. If you're still here, I expect your assurance that you've let him know you're okay."

Leaving the door ajar, Grace listened hoping to hear a promise to contact Ches, but none came. She left the house, her mind spinning with uncertainties of how she was handling the situation with giving refuge to Ches' daughter.

I shouldn't have said I wouldn't tell him. He needs to know Sunni's okay. He is worried about her. He has to be.

God, what can I do?

Grace didn't really expect an answer, though she mulled over the question as she drove to the hospital and began her duties there. It was a trauma day which meant any persons sustaining serious injuries including head traumas would be coming in to Regional. The chaplain was part of the trauma team, mostly to offer comfort and be the communication between the medical staff and the family as they waited.

She spent most of her day on the oncology unit, visiting each patient in their rooms.

One such patient, Marley King, a seventy-year-old man with colon cancer, waved her into the room.

"How are you today, Chaplain?" His eyes shone bright.

"I was just going to ask you the same thing." Grace paused at the sink to wash her hands. Finished, she threw the paper towel in the receptacle next to the sink.

"Word is I might get to go home tomorrow."

"Well, that is a good word, isn't it?" Grace sat on the chair next to Marley's bed.

"For sure. For sure. And in case they got some doubts, I've washed myself up real good and walked up and down the hall twice now." He winked at her. "Made a point that the doctors saw me. Even waved at 'em."

"Home is a good place to be."

"You got that right. If I could bottle that smell, I'd make a million bucks."

Grace tilted her head in thought. "Except for each person's home has a different aroma, I would think."

"Naw. Ain't no one's home smells as good as mine." He inhaled deeply as if the scent were there for him to enjoy.

"What's home smell like, Marley?"

"Oh. Fresh baked bread and furniture polish. The wife's night cream and 50 years' worth of living in the same house." The older man smiled, his eyes becoming unfocused as if he were seeing a far off memory. "Lot of loving and laughter in those 50 years. A lot of tears, too. I wouldn't trade 'em. Not one day. No ma'am, I wouldn't."

"You miss being home."

Marley blinked, and his gaze settled on her. "I'd pay a million dollars for a bottle of that home smell, if I had a million to pay. But since I don't, I just need to get there myself, and that means I got to convince the slew of doctors that parade through here that I'm well enough to go. You got a prayer for me to that effect?"

"I certainly do," Grace said.

When Grace took her lunch, she saw she had a missed call from Ches. She immediately called him back.

"Ches? It's Grace. I saw you'd called me."

"Oh. Yeah. I didn't really need anything."

His tight tone alerted her that something was off. Was he as upset as Sunni was from their argument the night before?

"You wanted to talk to me. That's enough reason to call."

"I suppose."

He didn't say more, and silence pervaded the call as Grace mulled over how she could respond. The affection she felt for Ches, and the heartache he must feel over his daughter spurred Grace to boldness.

"Ches, if you need me, I'm here for you. You can trust me, as I already trust you with my feelings, my....heart." Grace's chest ached as she said it. Would he understand what she was telling him? She hoped so, and she hoped not.

"I wouldn't mind having your heart, Sugar, except I haven't done too well with my own."

"Perhaps that is why you need mine."

More silence. Was this a rejection, or a quiet acceptance? If Ches were in the same room with her, she could see him, recognize the visual cues, but she only had his voice—or lack thereof—on the phone line.

"Trust me with whatever it was that made you dial my

number, Ches. Would you do that?"

Ches sighed. "Sunni didn't come home last night. We argued, and she left. That's nothing new, but her car wasn't in the garage when I left this morning, and I went home at lunch, and she still hasn't been home."

"She left you a text, though. Or a voice mail?"

"No. Nothing."

Grace looked at the clock on the office wall. She'd given Sunni a gentle ultimatum: if she were still there, she will have contacted Ches, or else lie to Grace that she had. What would Sunni do?

"Why don't you give her until supper tonight? If she isn't home by then, and you haven't heard from her, we'll figure out what to do."

"She's never not come home before."

"You're worried."

"She's a grown woman," Ches countered, perhaps trying to convince himself it was okay that his daughter was missing.

"In a sense, she's still your little girl, though. Trust that you've raised her well enough that she is somewhere safe, cooling off and calming down."

"She won't let this thing go about Cinnamon. He's gone. Why can't she just move on?"

"Maybe because she loves him. And she feels that you betrayed her when you sold him without her consent or knowledge."

"I am doing what is best to protect her."

What an odd statement. How was selling her horse protecting Sunni? However Ches had justified it, Grace didn't think exploring his reasons was appropriate over the telephone. She chose her words carefully.

"It seems to me that she doesn't want you to protect her. You've told me she's a grown woman. If you really believe that, then would you handle this in the same way?"

He let out a sound of frustration. "Probably not."

Grace waited for him to say more, but he didn't. "I'm with you in this. You're not alone."

A few seconds ticked by. Ches cleared his throat. "I've been alone for a long time now. Even before her mother left, I only had me to deal with it."

"Having someone to lean on is new to you. I understand. It's new to me, too."

"When have you needed me to lean on, Sugar?"

"Oh, riding horses and cars in ditches. But the biggest one so far was probably the hug outside of the chapel at the hospital. I felt so alone, overwhelmed by the loss of that family. I had been praying in the chapel. And when I walked out, there you were, an answer to my prayer, I think."

Though she didn't realize it until this moment. God had answered her prayer—provided someone there to comfort her and remind her she wasn't alone.

"You're not alone," Grace repeated. "I'm here, Ches."

"All right." In those two words, Grace felt something shift in Ches. The dam of self-reliance—cracked when he'd first called her earlier in the day—broke open. The waters of trust flowed forth. "I'll call you tonight."

Grace hoped that by the time she talked to him again, Ches would have some contact from Sunni, even if Grace had to nudge the young woman to do it. Sunni's car was still in her driveway when she arrived home a little after five. Inside, she found Sunni on her laptop at the kitchen table.

"Hi," she said.

"Hi," Sunni echoed.

Coming home to a warm body in the house felt nice, Grace decided. She washed her hands and poured herself a glass of water from the tap.

"Want something to drink?"

"No, thanks."

Grace drank from her glass and leaned back against the counter. "What did your dad say?"

Grace chose to ask the question in a way that assumed Sunni had contacted him.

"He said, 'ok.'"

Relief washed over her. "Good. He knows you're okay, and he acknowledged your text."

Sunni's eyebrows drew down. "How did you know I texted him?"

Grace shrugged. "It's your preferred communication. I appreciate that you let him know you were okay. Thank you."

"Why are you thanking me?"

"Because I care about your dad, and I don't want him to worry about you."

"You care about him."

"Yes."

"Care, as in you love him?"

The question made all the nerve endings in Grace's body jump. She could evade the question, couldn't she? But she didn't want to. Because if fear was keeping her from risking her heart, then fear was not going to win.

"I think so. I've never really been in love before, so I'm not sure."

"So, you letting me stay here is just your way of getting in good with him. Hoping he will love you back if you're nice to me."

Grace set the glass on the counter top and folded her arms. "You are welcome here, Sunni, and I'm glad you felt this was a safe place for you to be. That will be the case whether your dad and I are in a relationship or not. You will always be welcome here. But when you and your dad are upset with each other, you being here puts me in the middle, especially when you ask me not to tell him. I don't want to keep secrets from him. It could hurt him, and I don't want that." Coming over to the table, Grace sat down next to her. "I am coming to love you, too, and the woman you are becoming."

Sunni had been watching her with a burning intensity, but her gaze dropped. "My mom doesn't care about me. She took me with her when she left my dad, but after she got married again, she brought me back here and dumped me."

"It still hurts, doesn't it?"

Sunni took a shuttered breath and nodded once, her eyes still downcast.

"Are you a hugger?"

"Umm." Sunni sniffed. "I guess so."

"Stand up, then, and let me hug you."

Dutifully, Sunni stood. Grace followed suit and put her arms around the young woman, drawing her into her embrace. For a second—maybe two—her stiff posture demonstrated her discomfort, then she relaxed, leaned into Grace, and grasped her tightly. Grace decided she'd hold the girl until Sunni pulled away, and it was a good long time before that happened.

"Hugs are nice, aren't they?" Grace said dropping her arms.

Sunni laughed and wiped her eye. "You're goofy, but Grace, I really like you."

Grace prepared a meal with Sunni's help. They sat down at the table and ate. Grace realized how much she enjoyed having someone to share a meal with.

"You know, staying here is a lot more convenient to school than home. I can be sitting in my class in 20 minutes from your house. When I'm coming from Wren's Holler, it takes me an hour, and that's if I can get a good parking space," Sunni said.

Grace cut a portion of the baked chicken on her plate. "I'm glad it's convenient, but you need to work it out with your dad. Soon. Even though you've let him know, you're okay, I'm sure he's still very anxious because he doesn't know where you are." Grace waited until Sunni met her gaze. "Will you please talk to him and let him know?"

"Look. I texted him and all he said was 'ok.' He didn't ask me where I was or anything. I don't think he really cares. He keeps telling me I'm an adult. Well, shouldn't I be able to come and go as I please?"

"When you're part of a family, you let those who love you know where you are and how you are. That way, they know if you need help, or even prayers."

Sunni snorted. "My dad doesn't pray."

"Well, maybe not. But I do, and if I had a daughter, I would want to know what was going on in her life, where she was, who she was with, so I could pray for her specifically. And I also could know what she needed from me. Your dad isn't a big talker, but I do know he has a big heart."

"It doesn't feel like it right now."

"Be patient with him. If you possibly can. Give him another chance to show you he loves you. Would you do that for me?"

Sunni pursed her lips. "In exchange for letting me stay here?"

"No. In response to letting you stay here. Like a *thank you* to me."

Afterward, Sunni offered to clean up and Grace used the time to go visit her grandparents and check on them. When she returned, she saw Ches' truck in the driveway parking behind Sunni's car.

Oh, good. Sunni must have called him. Maybe they were working things out.

Grace sure hoped so.

She parked in the carport and entered the house. Sunni's raised voice met her.

"I don't! I want to know who has him!"

Ches spoke, but what he said was lost to Grace. She didn't want to appear as if she were eavesdropping, so she entered the room.

Ches and Sunni stood facing each other. Sunni's red face turned, anger written all over her. Ches also turned, his expression tight.

"Excuse me. I'll just go upstairs so you can have some privacy," Grace said.

"Why don't you stay there, Grace," Ches said in clipped tones though he was looking at Sunni. "You want to know what happened to Cinnamon? He's dead. You left the gate open. He got out, ran, and he was hit by a tractor trailer on Route 17. He's buried out in the back acreage."

Ches stalked across the room toward the front door. His flinty gaze pinned Grace at the bottom stair. "Has she been here the whole time?"

Feeling her heart burn to ashes, Grace nodded once.

A nerve ticked in his jaw. "You could have told me, but you didn't. You let me worry and wonder, and all this time...." He dropped his eyes and shook his head. Walking to the door, he opened it and left without a backward glance.

Ignoring the hole in her chest, Grace focused her attention on Sunni whose raised arms were in the posture as if she were warding off the awful news Ches had just delivered. She opened her mouth and gulped the air, then let out a gut-wrenching cry.

Grace rushed to her before she collapsed in a heap of grief and tears. Grace ushered her to the couch, holding the young woman and murmuring words of comfort. Sunni cried great heaving sobs demonstrative of a breaking heart. After a while, she quieted. Sniffing, she sat up.

"Is it okay if I stay here again tonight?" Sunni asked.

"Of course, it is."

"I think I'm going to go to bed then."

"All right, sweetheart."

Grace watched the young woman rise and go up the stairs.

Lord, please comfort this poor child.

****

Grace didn't attempt to contact Ches that evening, deciding he needed some time to process the episode which had occurred earlier. He was angry with her, of course. But would he let her explain to him her reason for not telling him where Sunni was? Would he allow her to apologize, because maybe Grace should have told him. But she had encouraged Sunni to let him know. Was that enough? Should Grace have done more? She went to bed without knowing the answers, sleeping in fits and starts, the look of betrayal on Ches' face stamped on her mind.

The phone ringing woke her up. Groggy, Grace picked

it up off the bedstead and squinted at the screen. This time, it was Meemee calling at six in the morning.

Probably not good.

Grace answered the call.

"Grace, it's Meemee."

The three words held fear and resignation. Something had happened. Something really bad.

"Grandpa. What happened?"

"He fell. We're at the hospital."

Grace wrenched the covers back and began sorting through clothes. "Regional, right?"

"Yes."

Hurriedly dressing, Grace then knocked at the other bedroom. "Sunni?"

Hearing a summons, Grace opened the door and stood at the threshold. From the light of the hallway, Grace saw Sunni in bed. She sat up in bed, wiping her eyes.

"I'm sorry to wake you so early," Grace said. "But I have to go see about my grandparents. My granddad fell. He's at the hospital. Try to rest some more. It's still early, child." Grace shut the door softly then picked up her purse from the chair and left.

Anxiety punched at Grace as she drove to the hospital. She'd gone ahead and put on her work clothes since nothing would be resolved by the time she was scheduled to work. Should she call another chaplain to cover her shift? Grace wasn't sure, so she waited to see what the morning would bring. Parking her car, she prayed for Granddad as she gathered her things and hurried into the building.

He was on blood thinners, so if he hit his head, it could be bad.

Very bad.

In the Emergency room, she looked on the large electronic screen for her granddad's name and saw he was in room 14. She turned heel and walked steadily to the room, breathing deeply, willing herself to be calm for Meemee. When she arrived at the room, it was empty. Not even a bed.

Lori, a CNA, walked by. Grace asked, "Where's Homer Larson, the patient in room 14?"

Lori paused. "CT, I think. Stroke Alert, right? What are you doing here this early?"

"He's my grandfather. Where's his wife?" They wouldn't have sent her to CT with him. She should be in the room waiting for him.

Lori shrugged. "Oh, honey. Don't know, but we'll find out." She grasped Grace's arm and pulled her toward the nurse's station. "The patient in 14, where's his wife?"

Buffy, the unit clerk, pointed toward the double doors down the hall. "Family room."

The department had two rooms designated for families of patients—usually trauma or critical care—when the staff were attending. Ironically, Grace's job was often to act as go-between to the families in these rooms and the medical room until the staff gave the okay for family to be present.

Even before Grace entered the room, she called out, "Meemee?"

Brenda appeared at the door, her expression drawn with worry. "Grace." The women embraced. "They let me ride in the ambulance, but I couldn't go in the room with him."

Grace walked with her inside the room and sat down next to her on the couch. "I know, Meemee."

Brenda's worried gaze sought Grace's, perhaps for an indication of what she knew. "Have you seen him?"

"No. Not yet."

"Will you go see?"

"He's not in the room. They're doing scans. Seeing if there is any damage. Do you think he broke anything? Did he hit his head?"

"I don't know about broken bones. He must have rolled out of the bed. Hit his head on the bedstead. So much blood." She shook her head.

"Was he awake?"

"Yes." Brenda held Grace's hand tightly. "But he was

174

so confused. He didn't even realize he was hurt. I know he is wondering where I am. Oh, Grace, my poor Homer." She shook her head. "I should call your father."

"No. Let's wait until we know something."

"All right. All right."

"I'm going to see if he's back yet." Grace stood. "Will you be okay?"

"Yes. Go on."

Grace nodded and hurried out of the room. Going to the locked double doors, she swiped her badge to obtain entry. The radiology department was to the left of the emergency department. This early in the morning, her granddad was likely the only patient there.

Striding down the hallway, she saw the door closed in the first CT scan room and the red light warned people should not enter. Nevertheless, the urge to go in was almost too much to bear. Grace leaned against the wall and waited, praying.

In a moment, she heard sound from within the room, and the door opened. Grace looked inside and saw Melanie, a nurse, pushing Granddad's bed toward the hall. A tech, dressed in black scrubs, stood at the doorway.

"Granddad," Grace said approaching the bed. A terrible gash oozed blood from above the hairline. Dried blood pooled on the pillow under his head.

Homer's closed eyes fluttered open. He looked at her, but no recognition appeared.

"It's me, Grace."

He closed his eyes again. Grace looked at Melanie. "He's my grandfather. He's on Coumadin."

"Do you know how much?" she asked.

"I can find out. His wife is here. I'm sure she has a list of his meds. He's got dementia. Can she see him?"

Melanie nodded. "Sure. We're in 14. Bring her back, if you want."

"Is Dr. Wainscott here?" Dr. Wainscott was the neurosurgeon for the hospital, and a very gifted doctor.

Melanie nodded, but didn't say anything. She knew

something, but she wasn't saying it, and whatever it was wasn't good.

Oh no. Oh no. Oh no.

"I should call my dad, then. His son."

Melanie cut her eyes to the right, then met Grace's gaze. "I would."

****

That evening Grace walked into her house feeling as if she'd been hit by a truck. Sunni stood next to the table and watched her.

"Is everything okay?" she asked. "With your granddaddy?"

Grace gave her what she hoped was an appreciative smile. "He's not doing well, but we'll see."

"Oh." She dropped her gaze. "Do you want me to stay? I was thinking about going home. I've run out of clothes, but I can stay here with you."

"No, honey. You go on. I actually came back so I could get a few things to stay at the hospital tonight. I'll be okay." Grace nodded, hoping Sunni didn't look too close at the sheen in her eyes. "You'll talk to your dad, won't you?"

Sunni sighed. "Yeah. I realize now he was just trying to make it better. He thought if I didn't know what really happened, it wouldn't bother me as much."

"Was he right?"

She bit her lip then shook her head. "No. I needed to know. It was... my fault. Dad had told me several times that if I didn't lock the gate, it wouldn't stay closed. He'd tried to fix it, but...." She finished the sentence with another sigh. "I need to show him that I can handle the truth. Put on my big girl panties."

Grace laughed. "Haley said something like that to me one time."

"Yeah. It's a phrase at our house about handling what life deals you, and taking responsibility. I need to show Dad I'm up for it."

"Sunni, I'm proud of you."

She shook her head self-depreciatively. "Don't be

proud just yet. It's easier to be calm when Dad and I aren't in the same room."

"We could call him and see if he'd come over here. Maybe I could act as a buffer."

"You've got enough going on with your granddaddy. We'll be all right, and Grace?"

"Yes?"

Sunni reached forward and hugged her. "Thanks for letting me stay here and for being so great."

Tears stung Grace's eyes at the unexpected gesture. She returned the embrace. "You're very welcome. Any time."

Sunni drew away. "I know you mean that, and it means a lot." A line appeared between her brows. "Have you talked to Dad?"

"No."

"You guys are okay, though, right? I mean, he's not mad at you because of me, is he?"

"Don't worry about it. We'll sort it out."

At least, Grace hoped they would. But she couldn't concern herself over it now. Meemee wouldn't leave the hospital, so Grace was going by their apartment to pick up some things for her as well. Mom and Dad were trying to get a flight in, but it would probably be tomorrow evening before they could get here. She wasn't sure it would be soon enough.

Granddad had a massive brain bleed. They had had to ventilate him shortly before noon, though by then Grace knew it was hopeless. He wasn't going to live, but Meemee was too distraught to let him die without his only son having the chance to say goodbye.

Grace knew all the words she'd said many times to families in grief. They ran through her mind, but stuck in her throat before she could utter them to Meemee.

After Sunni left, Grace gathered some things together. It was strange how bereft the house felt without Sunni—as if the building realized Grace was alone here.

But I'm not alone. Lord, you're with me. Help me feel you.

****

Ches stepped into the house, removing his hat as he did so. Wiping the sweat from his forehead with the sleeve of his shirt, he looked around for Sunni. In the two days since she'd been back, she hadn't said much to him, but the hostility she'd worn like an armor was absent and she'd made a point to eat meals with them. Was the newfound truce because he'd told her the truth about Cinnamon, or was it because of her time at Grace's?

Sunni sat at the table typing on her laptop. She looked up when he entered the room. "Want me to go get Haley?"

The offer surprised him. "No. I'll get her after I shower, but I'd like to talk first." He went to the sink and poured himself a glass of water. "That all right with you?" He turned around and saw she had pushed her computer to the side, but her gaze was on the table top.

Ches sat down. "I'm sorry for how I told you about Cinnamon. I was... surprised that you were at Grace's, and I said it without really meaning to."

"I'm glad you told me, Dad. I needed to know," Sunni said. Her calm voice surprised him again. He waited for her to say more, but she didn't.

He blew a breath out. "It was... a very tragic accident."

She shook her head. "I didn't lock the gate. It was my fault." Her voice broke on the last word. She blinked a few times, and looked out the window.

"You didn't lock the gate, yes. But you weren't the only one responsible. I should have replaced the lock instead of trying to fix it. And he was so bad about running. If he would stay close to the house, he would have been just fine, but the dummy never stayed put."

Sunni continued to stare out the window without speaking.

Ches searched his mind to think of something that would bring her gaze back to the room, some nugget of connection between him, her, and the horse they no longer had. "You remember that time Cinnamon got out and went into Matt Brown's barn and was eating his oats?"

Her mouth turned up in a smile. "Yeah." She turned to Ches. "Mr. Brown called over here and said he had a thief in his barn."

"I couldn't figure out why he'd call me and not the police."

"I'd braided a ribbon with the tag on it in his mane, and that's how Mr. Brown knew who he belonged to."

It was Ches' turn to smile as he remembered the tag on which she'd embroidered the moniker. "Sunni's Cinnamon."

She sighed, and a tear rolled out of the corner of her eye.

"I'm so sorry."

Finally, she looked at him, the sheen of unshed tears apparent. "Thanks, Daddy."

At once, she was in his embrace—his little girl. He bent his head and rested it on top of hers. Years. It had been years since she'd allowed him this close. It felt so good.

"I love you, Sunni. So much."

"Love you, too." Her words were muffled against his shirt.

He eased away. "I should have showered and changed so you wouldn't have had to hug all the dirt and dust of today's chores." He began to walk toward the living room door.

"I can get Haley."

"No. I'll pick her up later. I want to get cleaned up and start supper first," he said over his shoulder.

"Wait. I want to say something."

Ches turned around and waited. Sunni picked up her phone and, standing she approached him. "I found this app on my phone. It's a family app to know where everyone is. That way, if you worried about me, you can just look and see where I am, and you'll know I'm okay."

Shock caused Ches to narrow his eyes at his daughter. "Are you offering to put a tracker on your phone so I will know where you are every minute?"

"Yeah." She touched her phone then held it out to him. "See?"

He looked at the screen. It was a map with the house address in the middle, and a small circle with Sunni's name in it.

"It says I'm home, and I can put it on your phone and know where you are. It's a great way for us to keep track of each other. What do you say?"

Ches unclipped his phone from his belt. "I say great. Here. You can put the app in for me."

Sunni smiled, and Ches placed the phone in her hand. He pivoted, heading toward the living room and up the stairs, ready to get that shower.

"Have you talked to Grace?"

That halted his progress. He didn't turn around, just answered her from the threshold.

No, he hadn't. Her name brought back the stinging betrayal of her not telling him Sunni had camped out at her house.

"No. I haven't talked to her."

"How come? You're mad at her, aren't you?"

Ches turned around then. Sunni's arms were crossed over her chest, and she had one hip thrust out like she usually did when she was gearing up for an argument.

Fighting mode, he'd come to know it as.

He chose his words carefully, not wanting to damage the precarious peace they'd achieved this evening. "I wish she'd told me you were staying with her."

"I told her not to."

"Maybe so, but she wasn't bound by what you wanted. She made a decision to keep your whereabouts from me knowing how worried I was."

"So, you're breaking up with her because you didn't know where I was? Look. The app will—"

"Breaking up with her?"

"Don't you love her? Are you going to let some stupid little thing like this be your excuse to never speak to her again?"

Shock glued his feet to the floor. Love her? Don't you love her? What was Sunni talking about? Love her?

Love? Her? Grace? Love Grace?

He shook his head. "We... don't really have...."

What?

Putting his hands up in a gesture of confusion, surrender—something—Ches turned around again and headed to the stairs.

His life was overrun, overturned, overwhelmed by women of all ages.

They muddled his mind.

He needed a shower.

Later that night, he sat on the edge of Haley's bed. The book he had read to her lay beside him tilted at an angle made by her small legs under the covers.

"Now we say our prayers," she announced.

Yeah, he knew.

"You gonna say prayers with me, Pop?"

This had been a new ritual, begun about a week ago. Haley wanted them to recite together the prayer Grace had taught her.

As if he could do anything else when Little Bit asked him then looked at him expectantly. Love for her filled his heart. "Of course."

Dutifully, he closed his eyes and waited for her to begin. Once she did, he joined her, but opened his eyes to watch her as she prayed.

"Lord, I have passed another day, and come to thank Thee for Thy care. Forgive my faults in work or play, and listen to my evening prayer. Thy favor gives me daily bread, and friends, who all my wants supply; and safely now I rest my head, preserved and guarded by Thine eye. Amen."

He leaned forward and kissed her forehead. "Sweet dreams, Little Bit."

"Poppy?"

"Yes?"

"Can Miss Grace come over? I miss her."

His heart hitched a bit. Yeah. He missed her, too. She should have told him about Sunni, but he hadn't given her the chance to explain why she hadn't, had he? The brief conversation between him and Sunni earlier had given him some insight into his daughter. She seemed to be handling the truth about Cinnamon a lot better than he expected. He had withheld the information about Cinnamon from Sunni to protect her, but maybe he hadn't needed to. Maybe he had been wrong. Sunni had given him the chance to apologize. She had forgiven him, and for that he was thankful.

Maybe he needed to show the same consideration to Grace.

He owed her a lot. She'd saved his life, after all. Shouldn't he allow her the chance to explain her side of things without jumping to conclusions? And even if she had kept the secret from him, he could forgive her. He'd kept a secret himself, and Sunni had forgiven him.

He could do as much for Grace.

"I'll call her and see."

"Do you promise?" Little Bit asked.

"Pinky swear," Ches said extending his smallest finger as a pledge. The child smiled and hooked her finger to his.

When he walked out of Haley's room, Sunni stood on the landing propped against the rail as if she'd been waiting on him. She handed him his cell phone.

"You are going to call Grace, right?" she asked, letting him know she'd overheard his conversation with Haley.

"She lets you hide at her house, so you all are best friends now?" Ches muttered.

"She kept asking me to tell you. She said she didn't like not telling you, but she was giving me the chance to do the right thing. Don't you see, Dad? If she'd told you, then you would have been mad at me, but she was trying to make it so I could tell you myself. She gave me a deadline. That's why I called you. I didn't expect you to drive to her house like that. I just told you where I was because she said you'd worry if you didn't know and to let you know I was okay."

Ches watched Sunni, her expression appealing to him to believe her.

"Dad, seriously. Please call her tonight. Her granddaddy was in the hospital. That's one reason I came on home. I figured she had enough to worry about, but I think she could really use a boyfriend right now."

"Boyfriend?" The word was so absurd, Ches barked out a laugh.

"Man friend. Guy pal. Significant smoothie. Whatever. Just call her."

"You say her grandfather is in the hospital?"

"Yeah. I think it was serious, but she was trying to play it off like it would be all right, so will you call her? I'm worried, and the last time I texted her, she didn't respond back."

Once again women were calling the shots in his life—the little one he'd just tucked into bed and now the bossy one who had romantic notions about him and Grace. Not that he disagreed with her necessarily, but love?

The word jolted him even as he walked down the stairs and pulled his cell phone from the holder at his belt.

Loved her.

Did he?

He settled on the recliner and scrolled through his contacts until he came to her name. Anticipation of hearing her voice prickled his chest. No anger. No sense of betrayal. Only wanting to connect with her again.

Ches smiled. Yeah, maybe he did. Love her.

He touched her name and the green call icon. Two rings. Then three.

"Hello?"

Happiness blanketed him.

Loved her. Yes.

"Sugar? It's Ches."

"Oh. Oh, Ches." She made a gasping sound that almost sounded like a sob.

Ches sat up, knocking the foot rest down in a quick swoop. "What's wrong?"

She didn't answer, and determination to find her, help her, fix whatever it was urged him to stand. He went over to where his boots sat near the kitchen door.

"Sugar, I'm coming over there to you. Are you home?"

"No, I'm at Carter Funeral Home. Granddaddy died. I'm at his visitation."

"I'll be there in 40 minutes."

He ended the call. "Sunni?" he called.

She came down the stairs. "Yeah?"

"I'm going to see Grace. Her granddaddy passed. You don't mind staying with Little Bit, do you?"

"No. Not at all."

"All right. Call me if you need me."

In minutes he was traveling north on the highway. He became aware of a phrase—as a mantra—ricocheting along the walls of his mind.

Listen to my evening prayer. Listen to my evening prayer. Listen to my evening prayer. Listen to my evening prayer.

My God, I'm praying, he thought. To You.

"I'm praying to you," he said in the silence of the truck cab. "Okay, Lord, since I'm praying to you, help Grace. I believe I love that woman, and she's hurting, and I don't know what the heck I'm doing. Help her. Help me. Help us. Lord, help us."

****

Serene. Stay serene, and breathe. Don't forget to breathe.

Grace stood next to her grandmother, with Mom and Dad on the other side. They had positioned themselves near the entrance of the visitation room so they could greet people as they entered. And there were so many, a testament of Homer and Brenda's friendship and involvement in the community. Several co-workers of Grace's from work had shown up as well, including her boss, Jonathan Fitzgerald and Lucy Merton, another chaplain.

Lucy stood in front of her now. The other woman's gaze roved over Grace's face. "You okay?"

Grace nodded, but Lucy shook her head. "No, you're not. Can you break ranks for a moment?"

"I shouldn't." Grace glanced at Meemee. The woman looked more frail than she'd ever seen her.

Grace felt something on her elbow and looked down. Lucy had grasped her arm and propelled her forward.

No. She couldn't. Her family needed her.

"Just for a few minutes," Lucy said, continuing to pull her forward. Grace looked back at her family. Meemee, looking intently into the face of Alfreda Sanderson, her neighbor, didn't seem to notice Grace was leaving. Dad laughed, engaged in a conversation with a man she didn't recognize. Then, Grace was in the hallway with Lucy who led her by the arm up several carpeted stairs into a smaller room. Lucy turned to her, watching her.

"I'm supposed to be better at this," Grace said.

"Why?"

"Because I comfort people daily who are grieving."

"He was your grandfather."

Was. A lump formed in Grace's throat. She didn't like how everyone talked about him in the past tense. He is still her grandfather. Death didn't change that.

"Come here. Sit down," Lucy said, urging her to an ornate settee that looked too pretty to sit on. "I'll get you something to drink." Lucy strode toward another doorway, and Grace wondered how she knew this place so well. The solitude after being in the cramped mass of conversations in the other room felt odd, as if her ears could hear the air flowing in the quiet room. Her phone rang, and she pulled the device out of her pocket.

Oh. It was Ches. Was he still angry at her? Did she really want to talk to him now? Yes, she did. She slid her finger over the screen and put the phone to her ear.

"Sugar? It's Ches."

The sweet gravely tone and his special nickname caused her heart to hiccup. "Oh. Oh, Ches." Her voice broke at his name, and she attempted to quell the emotion threatening to choke her.

"What's wrong?"

Tears leaked from her eyes. She sniffed and pulled some tissue out of a box on the table next to where she sat. Dabbing her face, she opened her mouth to say she was okay, everything was fine, but the lies wouldn't form on her tongue.

"Sugar, I'm coming over there to you. Are you home?" The determination in his words calmed her.

"No, I'm at Carter Funeral Home. Granddaddy died. I'm at his visitation." She rushed the words out before another sob could work its way out.

"I'll be there in 40 minutes."

Okay. Okay. Ches will be here in 40 minutes. She closed her eyes and breathed in and out. Deep sustaining breaths to calm as she had counseled people to do who were anxious and upset.

Breathe. Breathe. Ches will be here in 40 minutes.

She carefully wiped under her eyes and tapped the tissue to her nose then stood.

"Where are you going?" Lucy asked walking back into the room with a bottle of water in her hand.

"I'm going back out there with Meemee. She needs me."

Lucy crooked her head then nodded. "All right, but I'm going to stay around a little while longer and pull you back out if you start to look peaked."

Grace didn't respond. She'd be fine. Ches would be here soon.

In less than the promised time, he walked through the door, a prominent figure several inches taller than anyone else. Wearing blue jeans and pale green T-shirt under a khaki jacket, Ches' gaze met hers. Grace surmised the jacket was an attempt to dress up the casual clothes he was probably already wearing when he'd offered the emergent visit.

He stood in front of her father and offered his hand. "Hello, I'm Ches Larson. I'm a friend of Grace."

Dad shook his hand. "Hi. I'm John Sutton."

"I'm sorry for your loss."

"Thank you. This is my wife Penny. Grace's mother."

Mom smiled up at Ches as he moved in front of her and shook her hand. "Aha," she said.

Ches crooked his head slightly, as if puzzled by her greeting, but then, in his charming, gentlemanly way, he smiled at her and said. "Pleased to meet you, ma'am."

"And I am pleased to meet you, Ches."

Oh, goodness. Please don't let Mom say she knows about him because of me.

He was already side-stepping toward Grace, his gaze roving over her, as if checking to see if she were okay.

She was. Now.

"Hi," he said.

Warmth spread through her chest. "Hi." She offered her hand to him, and instead of shaking it, he grasped it with his left hand, then leaned forward and kissed her cheek.

"You all right, sugar?" he whispered quickly near her ear before he stepped back, still holding her hand.

Grace nodded.

He nodded in return, squeezed her hand, then moved to Meemee. "Mrs. Sutton, I don't know if you remember me, but I'm a friend of Grace's. Name's Ches."

John leaned in toward his wife, seeking eye contact with Grace. "More than a friend, I'd say," he murmured. "Or am I wrong?"

"John. Not now," Penny said in a low tone.

John straightened. "He started it. Kissing her on the cheek in the receiving line."

"Of course, I remember you, dear. Aren't you sweet to come." Brenda gripped his shirt and pulled him down to her. She kissed his cheek. "Good to see you again, Ches." She looked at Grace. "Isn't he sweet to come?"

Grace concurred, catching the sidelong glance her mother shot to her father.

"Sign the book there, so we have a record of it." The older woman nudged him toward a podium with an open guestbook on it.

"Yes, ma'am."

"Such a sweet boy." Brenda patted Grace's arm. "I sure like him."

Grace studied the breadth of the man's shoulders, the chestnut with just a hint of auburn hue of his hair, and the burned brown swath of his neck showing above the collar of his jacket.

I sure like him, too, Meemee.

He walked on into the room, and then someone else entered, pausing in front of them, and Grace's attention moved away from Ches. From time to time, her eyes would scan the room, and she'd spot him. She acknowledged the comfort of knowing he was close by. This was what loving someone felt like. The comfort of being in the same room, even if you weren't speaking. Grace liked that.

The crowd thinned, testifying to the late hour. Grace walked to where Ches had settled on a couch. In front of him on the coffee table was an open photo album of Meemee and Granddad's. Grace sat next to him. Ches flipped to a photograph of Grace in a dress standing with Granddaddy outside of their church. Grace was probably fourteen when the picture was taken, and already as tall as Homer.

"You were a beautiful girl," Ches said.

Grace shook her head. "I didn't feel beautiful. Only tall."

Ches pointed to the girl in the picture. "She was beautiful. Still is."

Grace bumped her shoulder against his. "Thank you, Ches."

Ches took her hand in his. "I'm sorry about your granddaddy. I'm sorry I wasn't there for you when he was dying. I know how hard it is."

Grace leaned toward him and laid her head on him, staring at the photo in the open book. "There are all these platitudes people say. He's in a better place. He's not suffering any more. He lived a good, long life. Things like that, and I know they're right, but the truth is I love Grandpa, and I am going to miss him very much."

Ches put his arms around her and nestled her into his side. He didn't speak, just held her, and it warmed her, comforting the ache of grief.

Penny, Grace's mother, approached them. "It's time to go."

Grace straightened, and they stood. Nearly everyone had left. Her grandmother and dad stood in front of the casket side by side.

"Your dad is going to stay with Meemee tonight," Penny said. "Ches, I'll see you tomorrow." She hugged both of them and headed toward the exit.

"What time is the funeral?" Ches asked.

"Ten o'clock. But you don't have to come. Mom just assumed you'd come, but I know you're busy."

Ches ran his hands up and down her arms. "I know I don't have to come. I want to be here."

"Will Sunni and Haley come too?"

He shook his head. "I don't think so."

"They can, if they want to." They walked toward the door, Penny ahead of them.

A troubled expression ran across his face. "I don't think it would be good for them. Haley's so young, and Sunni"—he trailed off, shaking his head—"she's actually never been to a funeral. When my sister died, we didn't let Sunni go. It seemed like it would be too traumatic for her."

"It's actually good for children to see adults grieve and say goodbye. It helps them know death is part of life. It hurts, but it's something families endure together."

"Is that Chaplain Grace talking?"

"Yes, and also the woman who enjoys your girls. If they want to be here, I want them to be."

Since her dad had taken Meemee home, Grace's mom would ride with her. In the parking lot, she handed her key ring to Penny, telling her she'd be back in a few minutes. Ches had paused for the exchange, and when Grace approached him again, he lay his arm around her shoulders, tucking her into his side, and they walked to his truck parked on the curb on the next block. Being next to him comforted Grace, like they were two parts of a whole. This was what it meant to be a couple, to absorb one another's strength and sadness.

Grace liked it. She really liked it.

The truck's headlights flashed, and she realized Ches had hit the fob unlocking the doors. Regretfully, she moved away from him. Ches opened his door, looking at her as he did so.

"I don't want to go," he confessed.

Grace took a shaky breath. "I don't want you to." Oh, she absolutely didn't, but Mom was waiting in the car, probably watching them out here next to the street. She crossed her arms so she wouldn't reach out to him.

His eyes darkened, and then she was in his arms, completely surrounded by his warmth. All him around her.

I love him. I absolutely love him.

"I prayed tonight." His words reverberated against her hair.

Had she heard him right? She lifted her face. "What did you say?"

"I prayed tonight. Well, I've been praying every night with Little Bit. She makes me pray with her the prayer you taught her, and Grace." He shook his head and gave a brief laugh, "When I was driving over here tonight, it's like the prayer was going through my mind. I was praying without even consciously meaning to." His arms tightened around her. "When I realized what I was doing, I... I didn't stop. In fact, I started praying out loud. I asked God to help you, to help both of us."

Grace returned his embrace, her own heart singing in gratitude for what God had done.

"God answered your prayer then, at least about helping me. He sent you here tonight, and it has helped me tremendously. I was falling apart, but when you called me and you said you were on your way, I knew it would be okay because you'd be here with me. Thank you, Ches."

She stood on her tip toes and kissed him. "I love you so much," she whispered, then realized what she said.

Fear and embarrassment pricked the tender moment like a needle to a balloon.

Without waiting for a response, she dropped her gaze and broke away from him, hurrying to her car. She entered the vehicle, avoiding the gaze of her mother. With a quick glance to where she'd come from, she saw Ches still stood next to the truck, still faced her.

Probably wondering how he could kindly let her down. Instead of going to the front entrance, Grace turned to the left and exited through the back alley.

Because she was a coward.

Okay, so she loved him, and now he knew it.

"So, how's your project coming along?" Penny asked.

"My project?"

Penny crooked her head over her shoulder. "Ches. Your ongoing project."

"Oh." Grace had called him an ongoing project, hadn't she? "Umm. We're making progress." She hoped so, though telling him she loved him might have messed things up.

"Making progress, huh? Yes, I saw that."

Grace smiled, the embarrassment melting off her. "He makes me feel petite when I hug him. I love that about him."

"You love that about him."

"Yes. Yes, Mom, I do. I love him. I really love him."

"Does he really love you back?"

"I don't know, but he let me ride his horse. Haley, his niece, says that means he really likes me. And he came to the visitation tonight because he knew I needed him. That means something, I think."

"Yes, I think so, too."

****

When Ches arrived home, Sunni was waiting up for him. He told her about the funeral and asked her if she wanted to go. Without hesitation, she said yes. He asked what she thought about taking Little Bit, informing her what Grace had said.

"If Grace thinks it's okay, then, yes, I think Haley could go. If she starts to get upset, I can take her outside or something."

Admiration for his daughter unfurled in his chest.

"You are turning into an amazing woman, you know that?" Ches said. "I'm afraid one day, you're going to leave here and never come back."

Sunni gazed at him earnestly. "You'd like me to, wouldn't you? I'm 19 now. Old enough to be out on my own."

Ches chose his words carefully. He remembered what Grace had said. It was time he let Sunni know that this would always be her home. "Yes, you are old enough to leave, but this is your home. I'd keep you here forever, if I could. This farm will be yours one day, you know. I'd like to think you would want to stay here and raise cows and corn, but, you've got enough of your mother in you that you probably would rather live in the city. I understand that, Sunni. But you will always have a place here. Always."

To his surprise, tears welled up in her eyes, and she covered her face with her hands.

"Honey, honey, what is it?" Ches took her in his arms.

"You're just saying that."

"No. No, I'm not." Ches stepped back and tilted her face to him, so she'd see his sincerity. "I don't know what I did to make you think I don't want you here, sweetheart. You're my daughter, and I love you. Of course, I want you here with me and Little Bit. And if you want another horse, we'll get one. Maybe a gelding or a mare, so it'll stay put. I've already put a new lock on the gate, so that won't be an issue anymore."

Hope sprung in her face. "Are you serious? You'd get me another horse?"

"I think you're old enough to pick one out yourself. We can go talk to Gene Harrington. He knows several breeders, okay?"

She reached her arms around him and hugged him. "Thanks, Daddy. I'd really like that."

Ches patted her back and pulled out his handkerchief. He handed it to her. "Now, dry your eyes. I've got to pull out my suit. I hope it still fits me. I haven't worn it in a while."

"Do you think we could have a memorial service for Cinnamon? I was thinking maybe Grace could do it for us."

"We could ask her. I don't know what the rules are for that kind of thing."

Ches went into the kitchen and poured himself a glass of water. In a moment, Sunni joined him, her phone in hand. "I texted Grace."

Her phone dinged signaling a text. Sunni looked at the screen.

"Ah. She says, Pets are often our first teachers of loyalty, faithfulness, unconditional love, and grief. Not sure if you considered Cinnamon your pet, but I know that he must have been a dear friend. Of course, I will do a memorial service for him." Sunni looked at Ches and smiled, a tear fell down her cheek and she wiped it away. "Dad, I really like Grace. Have you ever thought about marrying her?"

Ches gave a surprised laugh. "Yes, I have. She told me the only way she'd marry me was if I was dying."

Sunni narrowed her eyes in disbelief. "She didn't say that."

"Yep. Of course, I think she was trying to get me to take better care of myself."

Sunni's fingers moved rapidly across the screen of her phone.

"What are you doing?" Ches growled. "You're not texting her, are you?"

"Just a little one." Sunni snickered.

"I wish the women in this house would quit bossing me around and let me take care of myself."

"Hello, Mr. Heart attack. You suck at taking care of yourself."

Ches shook his head at his daughter's lack of respect. He walked toward the door to go in search of his suit. "We're leaving at 8:30 in the morning. Be ready."

The next morning, Ches sat in a church in the family section. Grace sat on one side of him, Sunni sat on the other, and Haley was in his lap. Not only were they in the family section, they were on the front row.

With immediate family.

Grace's grandmother, then her dad, then her mom, then her. There were some cousins, but the family itself was small only taking up two pews total, including himself and his crew.

Ches wasn't exactly sure why he was sitting with immediate family, other than Penny, Grace's mother had gestured him to come forward and pointed them next to Grace. Assigned seats.

Grace wore a navy blue dress with lace on the bodice. Her red eyes and nose demonstrated she'd been crying before they arrived. When she caught sight of him, Sunni, and Haley, she'd smiled, tears glistening in her eyes. Haley had wrapped her arms around the woman's neck, and the Grace had returned the embrace, an expression of comfort showing on her face.

The preacher talked about Homer and the many things he'd accomplished in his life. Then he talked about the Resurrection, a promise realized now for Grace's grandfather.

Ches studied the closed casket, covered with a large arrangement of roses of every color, lying in state in front of the church.

It was comforting to know death wasn't the end, that there was a place where death had no hold, no power. A place, as Grace had said, where babies don't stay dead, a place where there's no pain. Ches liked that idea.

Grace moved against him, and he reached over and took her hand, intertwining her fingers with his.

She'd told him she loved him. So much.

Had she really meant it?

Did she love him enough to marry him then?

Even if he lived long after his 40th year?

God, please, if you let me live to be as old as Homer, or even if you don't, would you let me spend the rest of my life with Grace?

After the service, Ches was relegated into a limousine with the family to the cemetery. Haley, who had never been in a limousine, bounced in the seat and squealed.

Ches gave her a stern look. "Settle down."

"Oh, she's okay," John Sutton said. "It is exciting to ride in a car like this, isn't it?" He winked at Haley. "My dad would have loved to know you enjoyed being in this big car. He loved nice cars, didn't he, Mom?"

"Oh, my, yes, he did. Many a car show he'd drag me to. When we had our 50th wedding anniversary, he rented a stretch limousine for our party. You remember that, John?"

"Indeed, I do."

"Where is your dad?" Haley asked.

"He's in heaven. Maybe he's looking down on us right now smiling at this fancy car we're riding in."

"You think there's holes in the clouds so he can see?" Haley asked.

John laughed. "Absolutely, there is."

Once at the graveside, Ches opted to stand so that some of the elderly people in attendance would have a place to sit. Sunni stood beside him watching Haley who was admiring a butterfly who had lit on a blade of grass a few feet away. The service only lasted 10 minutes, and Grace and her family greeted each person, thanking them for coming. Haley and Sunni had wandered off, and Ches kept his eye on them as people dispersed from the awning set up by the funeral home.

Grace came up to him, the hem of her dress pressed against her legs in the warm breeze. He liked Grace in a dress. She had beautifully long legs, and surprisingly dainty feet shown off by the beaded sandals she wore.

"Hi," she said.

"Hi, Sugar."

"We're going to my house for lunch. People have been

bringing food by. I have enough to feed an army. Will you and the girls come?"

"Sure, we will."

They'd gone to the church, retrieved their vehicles, then gone to Grace's house for the traditional meal with food provided by the church community and friends for the bereaved family. Ches found the gathering wasn't somber, as he expected, but an opportunity to share memories and stories of Homer. He sat on a kitchen chair which had been moved to the living room where most everyone had gathered. When he noticed the absence of Sunni and Haley, he went to look for them, finding them on the screened in back porch playing checkers. Someone touched his arm, and he looked to see Grace.

"I appreciate you being here, Ches." She smiled at him, but there was a guarded look in her eyes.

His heart swelled with feeling for her. He leaned close to her, whispering. "I love you, too, you know. I hope you meant what you said last night."

Grace's eyes widened.

"Did you mean it? That you loved me so much?"

She nodded, the guarded look falling away, and joy replacing it. Her mouth turned up in the prettiest smile he'd ever seen. She circled her arm around his and leaned her face next to his shoulder. "Sunni sent me a message last night."

"Yeah, about Cinnamon?"

"Yes, and wondering if I'd marry you even if you weren't dying."

Haley picked up a checker and jumped two of Sunni's pieces. "For someone as old as you, you aren't very good at this game."

"That's because I'm letting you win so you won't cry. Now crown yourself, you checker queen."

Ches, reticent to look at Grace, watched the girls for a moment. Then worked up his courage. "What did you tell her?"

"I told her if you were dying, I'd marry you for her and

Haley's sake so I could help take care of them, if they wanted me to."

He risked a glance at her. "Is that all you said?"

"I said the living part was up to you." Grace let go of his arm and pivoted to stand in front of him. "So, what about it, Chesapeake Larson? Do you want to live for another 40 or 50 years?"

"I absolutely do. With you. As my wife. As soon as possible."

Grace shook her head, love radiating on her face. "I want a long engagement. I want to get married on your 40th birthday."

"That's almost a year away. Don't make me wait that long, Sugar."

"I just want to be sure you believe you're going to make it to 40."

"What will it take to convince you we should get married sooner?"

"We could start with an engagement ring, I suppose."

"Sunni? Grace and I are going out for a little while. Little Bit, she's in charge of you, so do what she says."

Haley and Sunni looked up at them from where they sat on the floor. "Where are you going?"

"We need to go shopping to buy an incentive for a short engagement," Ches said.

Sunni gasped. "Engagement? You guys are getting married?"

"Married!" Haley squealed.

Ches grimaced. "Keep your voice down. We're eating funeral food." He grasped Grace's hand in his. "Should I ask your dad first? Or is it incredibly rude to ask to marry his daughter on the day he buried his dad?"

"I think he knew something was up when you kissed me at the visitation last night."

"It was on the cheek. Sorry. I didn't mean to…."

"It's okay. They've already decided you're part of the family. You did notice my mom had you sitting with us at the funeral, right? The section reserved for family only?"

"Ahh, okay. Let's go make it official then."

The End

About Jennifer Johnson

The Greatest Love Story.... Has been and continues to be God's amazing love. This story unfolds amazingly every day of my life. I hope that in my books and in my work that I demonstrate my deep gratitude for that love. I write romantic fiction and Inspirational Romance. Find out more at **www.booksbyjenniferjohnson.com**.